By The Sea

By The Sea

VANNA NILAVAN

Translated by G. Geetha

Vitasta
LET KNOWLEDGE SPREAD

TAMIL NADU TEXTBOOK AND EDUCATIONAL SERVICES CORPORATION
LEARN THOROUGHLY

Published by
Renu Kaul Verma
Vitasta Publishing Pvt Ltd
2/15, Ansari Road, Daryaganj
New Delhi - 110 002
info@vitastapublishing.com

ISBN 978-93-90961-40-5

First published in Tamil in 1977

First Edition 2023
MRP ₹ 320

Editorial Assistance by Alisha Verma
Cover & Layout by Somesh Kumar Mishra
Printed by Chaman Enterprises, Delhi

TRANSLATION INITIATIVE OF THE TAMIL NADU TEXTBOOK AND EDUCATIONAL SERVICES CORPORATION

This is an initiative of the Tamil Nadu Textbook and Educational Services Corporation (TNTB & ESC) under the aegis of one of the announcements for the year 2021-22, by Honourable Minister for School Education Thiru. Anbil Mahesh Poyyamozhi to identify and translate into English, Tamil literary works, that they might enhance the reach of Tamil antiquity, tradition and contemporaneity and enrich World literature and to also translate significant literary voices from other Dravidian languages into Tamil. Both ventures are to be undertaken as either independent or joint publications with collaborating publishers.

PREFACE

There's so much to say. I'm not yet tired of standing in a corner watching everything endlessly. Like everyone else, I keep seeking, journeying, in the thought that, after all, there must be something worthwhile in this life. Having started to write, I have now arrived at a point when people look up and say, 'Listen, he is saying something.'

Nothing is inconsequential. Everything matters. And everyone is worthy. Men have been given this great thing called love. There are no obstacles to drawing closer to a fellow human being. I think that no matter how much we lose, there is also something to gain always. Like Shri Sundara Ramaswamy said, 'We gain something only by losing something' and this is proved to be true time and again.

As I have become one of those whose task is to write, I speak about writing and literature from my heart. Art is a matter of the heart; of one's sensibility; it is closely related to truth. A good artist never lies to the people. Art cannot endure falsehood.

Now, about this story: I must say something, mustn't I? The very thought of these Manalpattur villagers in this story fills me with wonder. If there is love in your heart, the words you speak become a magic chant. It appears to me that these Manalpattur folk speak a divine language. They commit murder; betray their own friend; the wife thinks of deceiving her husband. There are quarrels too. And yet these folk know how to be affectionate towards everyone.

The heart must rise above all pettiness, must find redemption; and literature can assist in this. I keep writing in the hope that someday I too could create a work that can affirm and redeem like Ka. Na. Subramaniam's 'Anbu Vazhi' – The Path of Love.

Kalyani (Vannadasan) and Nambirajan were the first fans and friends of this novel.

This novel was serialized in the 'Kanaiyaazhi' magazine. My thanks are due to its editor, Shri K. Kasturi Rangan and my friend, Shri Indra Parthasarathy, who took this novel from me to Delhi.

My heartfelt thanks to the Tamil Nadu Textbook Corporation (TNTB) for taking this book to a wider readership through their translation project.

Tamil readers—every one of them—will always remain my kindred spirits.

Vanna Nilavan

TRANSLATOR'S NOTE

Vanna Nilavan's *Kadalpurathil (By The Sea)* is a timeless classic that is read and discussed with the same fervour by the Tamil readers even today as it was back in 1977, when it was first published. It tells the story of Cruz Michael, an ageing fisherman, and his family—their teetering lives in a small fishing village as mechanized launches and trawlers begin to replace artisanal boats. As much as it captures the throes of a seaside village on the cusp of change, it is also an ode to resilience. We witness conflicts arising from generation gap, the onslaught of commercialism and the desperate need to hold on to a vanishing way of life. But we also have Philomi, who exhibits what the poet Jane Hirshfield calls 'the sinuous tenacity of a tree.' Every time she finds 'the light newly blocked on one side,' she quietly 'turns in another.' There is hatred, betrayal, avarice and lust. But then again, there is friendship, forbearance and love. Vanna Nilavan swings expertly between the regional dialect bursting with the flavourful lingo of the fishing community and the dispassionate, philosophical voice of the narrator as he tries to bring alive the sights and sounds of a seaside village while also pondering the great puzzle that human behaviour is.

Recreating these various speech registers in English and capturing the lyrical beauty of some of the lines in the novel was not always perfectly possible. What sounded good in Tamil emerged stilted or ungainly in English at times. I remember reading somewhere that translation is like dancing on a slippery floor. You have to be careful not to slip and fall while also making sure that the dance is graceful. While translating this book, I was often left wondering if I was not just dancing on a slippery floor but also with two left feet to boot. But to rephrase the delightful Polish poet Wislawa Szymborska, I prefer the absurdity of translating to the absurdity of not translating. Ever since it was first published, the novel has never once failed to make it to the list of must-read books in Tamil. I sincerely hope that I have managed to recapture at least part of the magic of the original. My heartfelt gratitude to Mrs. Mini Krishnan for all her efforts in taking this translation to a wider readership. My sincere thanks to the Tamil Nadu Textbook Corporation (TNTB) for bringing out this book as a part of its translation project.

1

'Why did you educate me then? I would've rigged a *vallam* and set out to sea to fish, like you. Why did you educate me?'

Sebasti didn't have the courage to speak to his *appachi* – his father – face-to-face. His appachi sat on a bundle of dried fishing net in the front yard. Sebasti sat inside, on the doorstep. It was from here that he spoke to his appachi thus. Philomi was turning over the *nethili* spread out on the sands in the yard to be sun-dried. Though Philomi's ears were tuned to the spat between her elder brother and her father, her eyes roved the street end. There was no sign of Samidas. She had so much to tell Samidas that day, so many matters lay in her heart. Every now and then, the breeze wafted the scent of the drying nethili into the house.

Sebasti's appachi, Cruz Michael, didn't answer him for a while; he stared vacantly at the sea cormorants and eagles flying in the sky and scratched his cheek. The steady rush and roar of the sea fell on their ears like the sound of pouring rain. They were born into that noise, grew up and died in its midst. *Kadal Ammai*—Mother Sea—was equal to

Marial and *Yesu* whom they worshipped. Sebasti was now demanding they change all that.

'*Elei*, I wished to educate you… and I did just that. What do you want me to do about it now? *Ei*, Philomi kutty, can't you see the cormorants circling overhead? Take that old net over there and fling it over the nethili.'

'Appachi… your wish and all that is right. Thanks to it, I'm a teacher today in Vepangattur. Else, I'd be on a vallam with you.'

'Elei, do you speak so lightly of riding a vallam, eh? If you are a teacher today, isn't that life a gift of these fish? You speak as if those setting out on vallams are hen-pecked cowards. You faithless wretch, born on Kadal Ammai's lap, you have the cheek to kick her!'

'Tch tch… it's been this same old ruckus these past two days in this house.' Cruz Michael's wife intervened. 'Elei, Sebasti, if he doesn't want to go to Vepangattur, why don't you leave him alone! He didn't go even when your sister Amalorpavam and her husband Puchikaataan called him. What can anyone do if he refuses so adamantly?'

'*Di*, you devil's daughter! Get lost! Look at her, butting in with her big mouth, the worthless wretch. You go to your son's house or daughter's house if that's what you want. There, you can even take that runaway slut, Philomi kutty with you. Just because your son called you, you are jumping to go, are you? As if some great misfortune has come over you here! This Cruz Michael knows so many in this *parakudi* who went to their son's house and daughter's house, only to return with a begging bowl in hand. Go, you homeless wretch. If you are dying to suffer, go with him. Michael's hands and legs are still strong, strong enough to launch a vallam single-handedly into the sea. Above all, there's Mother Mary. Only Kadal Ammai and the fish remain faithful to this Cruz Michael. You are all ungrateful wretches. Get lost… get lost! Philomi kutty, fetch that towel on the clothes line. Let me walk up to the market place,' Cruz Michael thundered angrily.

Even before Philomi could get past her annan sitting on the doorstep, her ammai- her mother- went in, fetched the towel and handed it to her. Cruz Michael took the towel from Philomi and flung it over his shoulder. He noisily pushed open the gate of the split-bamboo fence and stepped out into the street. Philomi stood petrified beside her annan at the doorstep and stared vacantly at her appachi's retreating figure. A greater anxiety wracked her. There was no sign of Samidas at all. She wanted to tell him about these recent happenings in her house. 'Where did this Samidas go? He promised not to set foot in the toddy shop, didn't he? Will he go there ignoring my words? If he does, it can only mean he doesn't love me.' The more Philomi thought about it, the more she felt like crying. At once, she ran into the house.

Sebastian didn't stir from his place. He had very big plans. With the money from the sale of their thatched house and vallam, he could strike up a partnership with the *Sayibu* and set up a cycle spare parts shop in Udankudiyur. That was his dream. He had even given his word to the Sayibu. As a first step, he must convince his appachi, ammai and Philomi kutty – all three of them – to settle down with him in Vepangattur. His wife, Theresa, had given her consent. She longed to go around, her neck bedecked with fine jewellery, like their village headmaster's wife. And for that, this measly teacher's job just wouldn't do. She knew that very well. After taking everyone with him to Vepangattur, he must speak to his appachi and persuade him to sell the house and the vallam. Sebasti had even found a prospective buyer. All said and done, wasn't Sebasti a clever teacher in Vepangattur?

The vallam belonged to his grandfather's time. It was Cruz Michael's contention that you could not get wood of such fine quality anymore. It was full of holes though, all plugged and patched up with scraps of tin. The words *Matha Thunai* were inscribed on its helm with tar oil. It was in Cruz Michael's appachi, Dasaiyya's handwriting. If put up for sale, the vallam would easily fetch six hundred rupees today. The house would fetch more than a thousand. Only appachi had to relent.

'What a fine appachi he is! Thoo!' Thrusting his head out, Sebasti spat in disapproval. He then took out a cigarette from his shirt pocket, placed it between his lips and shouted, '*Etee*, Philomi kutty, bring me a light for my cigarette from the oven fire.'

Ammai was in the kitchen, raving and ranting. Ammai yearned to go and live with her son more than anything. Her desires weren't dead as yet. Only last week, her *periamma's* daughter, Lizzy, had come visiting from Thoothukudi. Her husband held a job in the Customs office. They had just two children. It had been a day's visit but how they all strutted up and down, slipping in and out of new clothes by the hour. Instead of dressing up like that and going out to the church, shops and movies, what kind of life was this – fiddling and carousing with these stinking fish all her life! There was a cinema theatre in Udankudi. She could go watch movies there. Udankudi was just a mile away from Vepangattur. You could even go there and get back by foot. It was for these reasons that ammai wished to go to her son's house.

Philomi kutty had no interest whatsoever in going there. If she left this Manalpattur village, how could she meet Samidas after that? Could she bear to live without seeing him? When she went in to bring Sebasti a light for his cigarette, she softly asked her ammai, 'Does ammai wish to go with annan?'

Mariammai who was frying dried fish in an earthen pan turned around swiftly. Her face was inflamed with the heat from the cooking fire. She was seized by fear and anger that Philomi had read her thoughts very accurately.

'Yes, that's what I want. Are you going to rot away here then? Go on, stay here. Stay back with your appachi. Only I know why you want to stay here. You're worried you may no longer be able to go gallivanting in the woods and all over the seaside with that scoundrel Sami and that slut of his sister, Dorothy; that you may not find the likes of them in Vepangattur. Do you think I don't know about your goings-on, you shameless slut! Wait, wait, let your appachi come!' Ammai lashed out at Philomi, hitting her in a soft spot. Fire tongs in hand, she broke down, sobbing uncontrollably. Sebasti yelled out from the doorstep, 'Etee… how long will you take to bring me a light?'

'You daughter of the devil, why do you pretend to cry? Come and take these embers. Can't you hear him call?' said Mariammai.

Wiping her eyes, Philomi took the embers. When he looked up to take the fire tongs from her, Sebasti noticed her crying. He couldn't bear to see her so. 'Di, Philomi, why are you crying, uh?' he asked her.

Philomi didn't reply.

'Come, come. Don't cry. I'm going out for a while. When I come back, we must settle the matter one way or the other today.' Saying this, Sebasti went out.

Philomi kept crying.

'Only when this stubborn wretch of a girl stops her weeping and whining will this house prosper. What's your age and what tricks are you up to? You shameless wretch. How you strut around smiling, showing all your teeth, when you speak to that wastrel Sami, you wanton whore! You just wait. If I catch you talking to him again, I'll tell your appachi. If he hears of it, he'll cut you to pieces and cook you up. Cursed wretch, why do you still whine?' Seething with rage, ammai rushed from the kitchen, grabbed Philomi by her hair and banged her head against the wall.

'Ammai… ammai! Don't hit me, don't hit me… aiyyo… don't hit me,' Philomi screamed. Her desperate cries reached the street.

***

That night when everyone had gone to sleep, Sebasti broached the matter once again. He was lying on the *thinnai* facing the front yard. Lying on his side, his head propped on his hand, Sebasti continued from where he had left off in the morning, 'Appachi… I must return tomorrow morning.'

Cruz Michael lay on a string cot in the yard under the canopy of the vast open sky. The moonlight fell on the bamboo splits of the fence and their shadow streaked his face. Philomi was sleeping with her head on the doorstep. Mariammai lay curled against the wall to the west of Sebasti. Michael turned and looked towards the house. In the soft glow of the night lamp, he could see Philomi's sleeping figure. How peacefully she slept; how graceful she looked.

'Such a tiny little thing this child was. How big she has grown now,' he mused. 'Hmm... seems only yesterday this kutty was wandering about the seaside with the other children of the street, picking shells and cowries.' Sebasti cut Cruz Michael's reverie short.

'Appachi, you haven't said anything. I told you I'm leaving tomorrow morning,' he repeated softly.

'Mm…? What did you say? Are you leaving then? Elei, tomorrow is a holiday, isn't it? Why don't you take the night bus instead?'

Their conversation always began that way, very amicably, without any fuss. But willy-nilly, it heated up.

'No. Not that I can't stay but I've told my wife I'll be back on Sunday. I've some work back there.'

'All right, leave then. Remember to take some dried fish from your ammai.'

'Mm. The matter I spoke about this morning…'

'What's that? What matter?' Cruz Michael asked brusquely.

'Kayal Pattinam Sayibu is going to set up a cycle shop and a radio shop. I've given him my word that I shall put in some money too. You needn't go fishing on this vallam any longer. You can all come with me to Vepangattur. I've found a nice groom for our Philomi kutty. My wife's annan's son- you know him- I think he's the right match for her. I've already spoken to them. It's all more or less settled. After selling this house and vallam…'

'Elei, Sebasti, you'll be in trouble if you bring up that topic again. You may talk of anything except that. Even if all of you pack your bags and leave, I shall never leave this Manalpattur village. This Cruz Michael's body must be buried in the churchyard here and that's that. So long as there's life in this body, I'll ride out to sea on my vallam and cast my net.' Cruz Michael shouted like one possessed.

Ammai who heard bits and pieces of the conversation muttered in her sleep. Startled, Philomi got up, and sat hugging her knees.

As Mariammai had given her an earful that morning, she had not gone to see Samidas that day. Poor thing, she was besieged by thoughts common to her age.

'Then consider that from now on there are no ties whatsoever between you and me.'

Cruz Michael felt as if someone had heaped fire on him. Must his beloved boat be subjected to such a trial? How could he bear to stay alive without riding his vallam, without casting his net?

'Elei, did I educate you only to hear you speak like this? What can matter more than a teacher's job, tell me? You're saying you're going to set up a business with some Muslim fellow. What will you do if everything comes to rack and ruin? Tell me!' He spoke in a pleading tone. Sebasti was his son. Wasn't he his own blood, all said and done?

'Why talk of all that? Sell everything and come away with me. Am I going to abandon you in the streets? Don't you have any faith in your own son?'

'Elei, if you're so adamant, go ahead and sell this house. Let the vallam remain as long as I live. It hasn't been long since we came by this house, but the vallam is our ancestral property. Leave me and the vallam here. The *paravan* is not born to do business; he is destined to row his vallam. A paravan is born by the sea and must die at sea. When I die, the pastor will let you know. You can then come here, bury me and leave. Go away all of you, leave! You can pack off even tomorrow if you wish. Do what you wish with the vallam after I'm gone.' Cruz Michael turned around and lay with his back to Sebasti. There were tears in his eyes.

Sebasti didn't utter a word to him after that. He lay on his back, staring at the roof, as if mulling furiously over something. His eyes reflected the severity of his ruminations. Philomi lay awake. Near her, her ammai was dead asleep. Through a small window on the western wall, a pool of moonlight fell into the house.

A whiff of talcum powder she had applied that evening rose from her face. When she was a small child, Philomi would simply curl up on her mother's lap and fall asleep in a moment. These days she was not able to sleep like that.

What was Samidas doing now?

Somehow, she couldn't meet him that entire day. Was he lying awake like Philomi? She wanted to believe he was lying awake too. The thought made her happy. Yes, he must be awake too, like her. He wouldn't be able to sleep either, for he hadn't met Philomi that day. And like her, he must have spent the whole day in a state of torment. But he was a man, wasn't he? Had he wished, he could have walked up to Philomi's house. But he hadn't. Could it be said that he hadn't been thinking of her simply because he didn't come searching for her? How could he not think of her? And yet, he hadn't come that day.

A lone crane cried out as it winged its way across the sky. It must have lost its way and missed its nest. Philomi got up, went to the window and looked out. The clouds were drifting to the west of the sea, like fluffs of cotton. Her chest heaved. She opened the backdoor and went out. No other sound could rouse Mariammai from her slumber but somehow, she always stirred awake the minute she heard the door creak.

'Who's that?'

'It's me, ammai. I'm going to the backyard.'

'When you come back, remember to bolt the door before you lie down to sleep.'

'Mm… ammai.'

The yard outside the backdoor was very long. As soon as you got down the doorstep, your feet touched the sand.

In the western corner of the yard, close to the fence, stood a well. Below its parapet lay a bucket, a rope around its mouth for drawing water. The area around the well was spotlessly dry. The narrow open cement drain that ran around it was encrusted with fine sand blown by the wind. There were four or five *vaagai* trees in the yard; a belt of coconut palms along the length of the fence. Bathed in the moonlight, everything looked beautiful. When her thatha-her grandfather – Dasaiyya had been alive those coconut palms had been his beloved children. These days, Philomi watered them only once in a while, that too only when Mariammai shouted at her for not watering them. Whether or not they were watered, the trees remained faithful and continued to yield. She pictured her thatha, the end of his *lungi* hitched up and tucked at his back, shuffling among the trees, bearing a bucket of water.

How her thatha had lavished all his affection on her! Philomi liked him more than anyone else in the family. It was with her thatha that she went to church every Sunday ever since she could remember. As a child, she used to walk clutching his rough, calloused hand. The hair all over his swarthy arms, legs and head had turned white. They lay in thick curls on his arms and chest. The previous Christmas, he had tottered all the way to the church for the last time holding her hand. Every step of the way he had kept repeating, 'Such trouble for my Philomi kutty because of this thatha, mm?'

'No thatha, not at all.'

'May you live well my child.'

How kind and loving her thatha had been. Walking up to the fringe of the backyard, Philomi stood gazing at the vast expanse of the sea. Black, moss-covered rocks that jutted out of the sand all along the shore glistened in the moonlight. And there were coconut palms- endless stretches of coconut palms as far as you could gaze. The fishing nets that had been hung between the trees to be dried swayed in the breeze. A paravan was tottering along the church, singing some song. The toddy shop was located not far away, in the direction he came from. For a long time, Philomi stood gazing by the fence, her hands clutching the bamboo splits. She then turned quietly and walked towards the house. Suddenly, she felt very weary.

What was Samidas doing now? Once again, she remembered him.

Only when she opened the backdoor and entered the house did it strike her that her annan, ammai and appachi were very much inside the house, all of them fast asleep. A while ago, she had felt utterly lonely, her heart heavy with a nameless sorrow. She bolted the door as her ammai had asked her to and lay down to sleep. But she didn't think she could sleep.

'Why is this annan so stubborn?' she thought. 'For that matter, even appachi is unrelenting. Annan is dreaming big. Ammai wants to go with annan. For all her age, ammai hasn't lost interest in dressing up. She wears blouses with such plunging neckline that the straps of her bodice could be seen.' Seized by intense loathing, she turned to look at her ammai, who lay sprawled on the floor, her clothes all askew. Lost in thought, she also looked at her appachi who lay on the cot in the front yard. 'What a good man appachi is! He has a nasty temper that flares up every now and then, but then his anger always disappears just like that, without a trace.' She wanted to get up and go to her appachi; to nestle close to him and sleep with her arms around his neck.

2

In the morning Sebasti and Cruz Michael didn't speak to each other at all. They avoided each other like bitter foes. Up long before the rest of the family, Cruz Michael still sat on his cot. He didn't go to sea that morning. It was a Sunday. Usually, very few ventured out to sea on Sundays.

During such squabbles, it was customary for Mariammai to side with her son. It was no different today. Sebasti was ready to leave for Vepangattur by the first bus of the morning. His ammai urged him to have some gruel before he left. She served coffee to Sebasti, but asked Philomi to take the coffee to Cruz Michael who sat in the front yard. Careful not to spill the coffee, Philomi got down the steps gingerly and went to her appachi. She stood in front of him and called out, 'Appachi… appachi… appachi.'

'Um…'

'Here, your coffee…'

'Leave it there.'

'It might get spilled…'

'Leave it there if you can. Else, take it back to that adulteress. Go.'

'Looks like appachi is sick at heart. You've told him, haven't you, that you won't go? Must you take his words to heart? Why, the whole village knows that Sebasti is hen-pecked. Cast it all aside, appachi. Your coffee will go cold. Shall I leave it here on the thinnai then?

'Mm… mm.'

'How annan and ammai joined forces and tormented appachi,' Philomi thought to herself as she placed the coffee glass on the thinnai. Just as she was about to enter the house, she heard the sound of the fence gate being opened. Philomi turned to look. It was Isaac, their neighbour. On seeing him, she turned her face away sharply. Isaac smiled as he sauntered into the yard.

'What's this… what do I see? Philomi kutty is so full of concern for her appachi. Look at her bringing him his coffee and all. Go on, go on. Michaelu, did you see that? No wonder they say a man must have a daughter.' He hitched up his lungi, tucked it between his thighs and plonked down on the cot beside Cruz Michael. The cot creaked loudly under his weight. Placing his forefinger and middle finger close to each other on his lips, he thrust his head forward and 'plich!' – he noisily spat out the betel juice he had been holding in his mouth. Cruz Michael sat lost in his thoughts, as if he hadn't noticed him at all.

The church bells pealed for the morning service. Inside the house, Philomi opened a clothes trunk, looking for a sari she might wear to church. A strong scent of naphthalene balls and talcum powder hit the air. She took out a valampuri conch, from between the clothes. It was a very rare conch bearing clockwise whorls. Samidas had given it to her. Every time she opened that trunk, her hands would instinctively cast about for it first and retrieve it. She now held it aloft and rubbed its back against her cheek. Hearing footsteps in the passageway all of a sudden, she stowed it hurriedly inside the trunk and turned around. It was Sebasti.

'Philomi kutty, aren't you going to the church today?'

'Mm… I am!'

'Where's ammai?'

'She's inside, where else?'

'All right, if you're getting ready, make it fast. I'm going to the church too. I'll catch the bus later on.'

Philomi didn't say anything. She rummaged through the clothes trunk wondering what she should wear. Sebasti shook out a dhoti from the clothes line so that he could change into it. In the front yard, Isaac was chatting away loudly with appachi. Philomi went on to change her sari by the window facing the yard. A little away from her, Sebasti was tying his dhoti. She was slipping her blouse on, when she noticed Isaac gaping at her through the window. At once, she slammed the window shut.

'Why do you slam the window so noisily?' Sebasti, who was buttoning his shirt, asked her.

'Appachi entertains all sorts of scumbags in the house and chats them up. He only knows to bicker and quarrel. Doesn't know the world one bit!' Philomi muttered.

When they were about to leave for the church, just Sebasti stuck his head into the kitchen, where ammai sat cooking. 'I'm off to the church. Philomi kutty is also coming with me.'

'Who? Philomi, eh? I know, I know. She would have dolled herself up and got ready at once. To see that fellow, what else? Never thinks of lending me a hand here. You don't seem to chide her either.'

'Why do you keep cursing that poor girl? After all, I only said I was taking her to the church. Where's the need to carp so much? Curse this family, bickering and brawling for every little thing!'

At that instant, Sebasti detested each and every one – his appachi, ammai, his akka Amalorpavam, Philomi Kutty; he was even angry with his wife in Vepangattur. Philomi stood leaning against the wall, her eyes riveted on the roof. Ammai's stinging words had brought tears to her eyes. She could take harsh words from anyone else, but one word from her ammai and tears rushed to her eyes.

Sebastian, who went up to the doorstep, turned around with irritation, 'Ettee... are you coming or not? These people – they care nothing about church or chapel. Are you going to rot and sink in the mire with these fiends? Etee... I'm talking to you, don't stand there like that.'

Philomi didn't move. She stood leaning against the wall, weeping. Sebasti couldn't bear to see her like that. Wasn't she his dear Philomi, all said and done? Wasn't she the Philomi he had amused and played with, his little Philomi, who had come running naked with him to the seashore to pick shells and cowries?

He walked up to her gently and wiped her eyes with the end of her sari. He stroked her head fondly. 'Look at you, crying like a baby… there, there, aren't you my dear little one! Now stop crying. Come, let's go.'

Picking up the Bible from the window ledge and hugging it close to her chest, she followed him. When she shut the gate of the bamboo fence behind her, she heard Isaac's loud cackle. 'Michaelu, just look at these two… going to church promptly like good children!' She glared at him through the bamboo splits and hurried behind Sebasti.

When they went past Samidas' house situated on the church street, she craned her neck towards the passageway of his house. The front door was shut. Four or five children were standing in front of the house and one of the boys cried out, 'Philomi akka is going to church!'

Perhaps, he had left for the church very early. Didn't he tell her, 'From now on I'll come to church on Sundays regularly?' Would he fail to turn up?

Sebasti and Philomi didn't speak to each other till they neared the church. She threw a casual glance at a group of young men standing at the entrance, searching for Samidas among them. After all, wouldn't she be able to spot her Samidas, no matter how big the crowd? Hoping to find him inside the church, she covered her head with the end of her sari and walked in, with lowered head. 'Philomi kutty, if you come out before me, stand at the entrance and if I happen to come before you, I'll wait for you here,' Sebasti told her softly. It was always that way. Whenever they came to church together, he always spoke to her in a gentle voice, audible only to her. An indescribable tenderness and brotherly affection saturated those words. As he walked in, she looked at him affectionately from the corner of her eyes.

'But for his temper, this annan is a good fellow. If only he never grew angry… he has inherited appachi's quick temper,' she thought. By the time she went in and found a seat, the service had begun. As soon as she sat down, Ranji walked in and sat beside her. Ranji nudged her gently in the stomach and Philomi turned to see who it was. Unable to express her surprise in the quietness of the church, she clutched Ranji's hand tightly and whispered, 'Ranji, Ranji is it you?' She forgot all that had weighed her heart down until a moment ago and a new happiness flooded her being. Just looking at Ranji made her happy. For that matter, who did not feel happy seeing Ranji? Ranji was joy incarnate.

Ranji was married and settled in Uvariyur. Like Philomi, she too was dark-skinned. She was robust and strapping, like a man. Her dusky face lit up beautifully whenever she opened her mouth to smile. Even Philomi used to tease her, 'Ranji, your man must have agreed to marry you only after seeing your smile. Else, would anyone come forward to marry a pitch-black creature like you?'

Her smile was not the only reason why the man from Uvariyur had come all the way to marry her. Ranji's appachi had promised to leave his vallam to his son-in-law after his days.

After the service, Ranji and Philomi were the first people to come out. Philomi searched for Samidas among the menfolk. When they emerged from the church compound, Sebasti joined them. Seeing Ranji there surprised him no end.

'Is it you, Ranji? When did you come from Uvariyur? Has your husband come with you?' he enquired.

For a while, Ranji didn't answer him at all but kept walking with lowered head, glancing at him out of the corner of her eyes. Memories stirred alive in her. Though she was someone's wife now, she couldn't forget Sebasti – this Sebasti who had endeared himself to her with his unfettered passion and playfulness. She struggled with her memories, unable to push them aside.

'Ranji… di, Ranji! Aren't you going to say something?' Sebasti asked her again.

Tears stung her eyes. She shrugged her shoulders, startled by the past that had taken hold of her so suddenly. 'Mm? What did you ask? He hasn't come; he stayed back. Our roof needs to be fixed. Besides, he has to supply fish to his regular traders.'

As soon as she started speaking, Sebasti's heart was no longer with him. Like her, he too stood lost in the memories of the childhood he had spent with her. Her voice carried him back in time to those days. Ranji took leave of them at the end of the street. None of her words fell into Sebasti's ears. Philomi, who had hoped to see Samidas, couldn't meet him. She walked quietly beside her annan. When they neared Mahmood's tea stall, Sebasti said, 'Philomi kutty, you go home. I'll just go up to our schoolmaster's house and be back,' and started walking towards the school street, not waiting for her reply.

Suddenly, Philomi was swept by a feeling of intense loneliness. She was already feeling wretched that she couldn't meet Samidas. And now, to worsen things, Chella Kutty, who teased her wherever he saw her, stood in front of the tea stall, making merry with a bunch of friends.

'Elei… look here, all of you. There goes our village beauty,' he shouted and a loud ripple of laughter followed. Philomi felt angry and irritated with Sebasti, appachi, ammai and even Samidas, for no reason at all.

Sebasti, who said he was going to visit the schoolmaster, was actually headed towards the toddy shop. Whenever he was overcome by memories of Ranji, he simply couldn't get on without a drink. As for Ranji, the very sight of Sebasti left her dazed and empty. At such times, all she wanted to do was just sit and stare at the sky.

When Sebasti reached the toddy shop, Isaac and Cruz Michael emerged from the shop, drunk to the hilt. Sebasti still hadn't picked up the courage to drink in front of his appachi. He stepped aside and waited near Ramaiyya Chetty's shop. Though Isaac was drunk, he was quite steady but appachi was a sorry sight. He lurched unsteadily and kept rambling incoherently.

'Dei… Isaac, my son says if we give my vallam away and set up a shop, we can grow rich. Crazy fellow! Whose property is that vallam, eh? Isn't it my grandfather's? That adulterous wretch – my wife – she says I should sell this vallam for my Philomi kutty's marriage. Filthy scamps! Both have their eyes on the vallam,' Cruz Michael poured all his grief out to his friend Isaac.

Not wishing to go to the toddy shop after that, Sebasti started walking down the road along the seashore towards churchyard. Grass had sprouted between the gravestones after the recent rains. Two half-burnt candles and an empty incense box lay on the grave of Valatti Paattan, who had passed away just last month. Perhaps, those candles had quivered and died half-burnt, fearing Valatti Paattan, who hadn't relinquished his authority over the village till his very end. All his life, Valatti Paattan had wielded power. For a long time, Sebasti sat under the *manjanathi* tree there. At a distance, the sea moaned. It sounded like a woman wailing over her endless miseries.

3

Sebasti left for Vepangattur that afternoon, promising to come back the next week. He hoped his ammai would somehow bring his appachi around by then. He was very disappointed that he hadn't been able to drink toddy that day. In Vepangattur, he could not even think of toddy, leave alone taste it. His wife wouldn't spare him if she came to know of it. He wouldn't have been reduced to this state if only he had married Ranji, he thought. But what to do? All that we wish for and pine after – do they come to pass? Once he went to Vepangattur, he would even forget Ranji.

Cruz Michael hadn't returned home even by the time Sebasti left. Perhaps, he had swilled some more toddy to drown his sorrows, and was lying in some coconut grove or under the fishing boats. The paravans in the village were all hooked to toddy. Father, son, grandfather – everyone drank without disparity. Only small children and young girls who had come of age weren't habituated to drinking. Even young boys, once they started setting out to sea, took to toddy. No one considered it offensive. The menfolk toiled hard; they fought with the vast, shoreless sea. They drank till their aching bodies were soothed. It was a necessity, or so they believed. Some of the women drank too. Philomi's ammai, Mariammai, drank. Women like Elia, and Pedro's wife Rebecca drank too. Of these women, only Rebecca ranted foully once she grew tipsy. She shouted such obscenities that her neighbours sniggered. This very same Rebecca also occasionally went to church.

In the afternoon, after Sebasti left, ammai stretched herself out in the hall and fell asleep. The roof of the house badly needed mending. It was years since it had last been thatched over. The wind had knocked loose a few fronds and they were fluttering, threatening to take off. Speckles of sunlight fell on ammai's fair legs through the holes on the thatch. The hair on her legs stood out in that light. Philomi sat down to eat, but she couldn't swallow a morsel. Something bore down her heart, choking her. It was perhaps her annan's newfound wish. There were no other children in the house after her. On several occasions, Philomi had longed for a younger brother or sister. Even now she wished she had a younger brother with whom she could wander about the seaside, gathering shells. Today she had felt sad that she didn't have a younger sister. The dried fish curry lay untouched in the pot. Hearing footsteps, she craned her neck towards the front yard. Isaac was helping appachi lie down on the string cot.

She rinsed her plate, put it away, went to the passageway leading to the front door and sat on her haunches. Inside the house, ammai sighed and turned in her sleep. Appachi lay on the cot, his lungi all askew. He was blabbering with his eyes shut. The skies were cloudy, threatening to rain.

Appachi would probably not go out to sea now. The fishing nets that had been hung out to dry on the fence the previous day still lay there. Perhaps, appachi might set out to sea in a little while. Anyway, there was still time. He might grow sober before that.

Philomi felt embittered. It seemed to her that a string of bitter happenings that left her feeling lonely and aloof kept coming her way lately. She stared at the sky. Large flocks of sea cormorants were flying overhead and huge king eagles were circling the sky by the sea. Above everything, rose the din of the sea. It absorbed her being. Whenever she was distressed, it was the relentless and reassuring roar of the sea, resounding in every nook and corner of the village that she heard. And whenever her thoughts and feelings shrivelled up and her heart grew empty, the sea rose before her eyes. How many forms it assumed and how many images it brought to her mind. The sea that brought the vallams and other country boats to the shore at dawn; the sea that swept up shells and small conches along with the white surf for the children of the parakudi; the sea by whose shore she had waited as a child with her akka Amalorpavam, basket in hand, watching her appachi's vallam come ashore. She remembered one thing after the other.

It was this seafront and her dear Samidas her Sebasti annan was asking her to leave. And for all you know, appachi might give his nod. A glass of toddy was enough to melt appachi's heart. He would do anything for it.

Meanwhile, next door, in Isaac's house, the usual fracas had begun. Isaac's full-throated voice grated on the ear like an elephant's loud trumpet. He was probably thrashing his wife. She caroused with a secret lover when he was not around or so he said. For a long time now, he had been flinging this accusation against that poor girl. Catherine was an exceptional girl born accidentally in the parakudi; a meek creature who didn't even know how to parry the abuses of other women in order to draw her share of water from the church well. It was on her that Isaac heaped indignities every day, running off at the mouth. It was this poor girl that he pounded black and blue. So many times, Philomi had heard her whimpering all through the night. Wasn't this a great injustice? And yet, didn't Kadal Ammai remain a mute witness, unable to put an end to it? Isaac's launch didn't capsize and he didn't disappear into the sea. Didn't the fisherfolk always say that Kadal Ammai was very patient, like mother earth?

Isaac's plans were very devious. By beating up Catherine day after day, he hoped to chase her away and marry Philomi kutty. Isaac knew that even if Cruz Michael didn't consent to anything else he might offer in exchange for marrying Philomi, he would certainly give in, were he to proffer his beautiful launch. Isaac was a tenacious fellow. Even if he desired a hundred Philomis like her, he would go on and carry out what he wanted. That was how, living amidst those poor paravans, he had still been able to buy a launch.

The clouds were fleeting westward in great clusters. Piercing the clouds, a rainbow had risen like a colourful arrow someone had shot across the sky.

****

Cruz woke up in the evening. He sat ruminating for a long time on the cot. Philomi was mechanically removing the fishing net that lay on the fence, taking care that it didn't get caught in the bamboo splits. She folded it carefully so that it could be carried easily to the vallam. She then went to the well to draw water. The pastor and Rosario were walking through the coconut palms towards the church. They were busy talking. Rosario was the pastor's favourite in the village. The pastor believed him to be the most upright fellow in the whole village.

Ammai had woken up at last and was moving about in the kitchen. Cruz Michael must have woken her up. Left to herself, Mariammai usually slept until the next morning when he returned from the sea. A good wife didn't sleep like that, thought Cruz Michael. She would be awake, praying to God till her husband returned home safely. 'May there be no waves on the sea. May the fury of the winds abate making it easy to catch fish. The vallam must not hit the rocks and capsize. More than anything, may there be a good haul so that our lives may prosper,' so would every *parachi* implore when the men folk set out for the catch. Even Mariammai had prayed fervently when she and Cruz Michael had been newly-weds. Now, her sleep ruined everything. What could she do? In any case, just because she didn't pray, the sea didn't rise angrily with a deafening roar and submerge Cruz Michael's vallam. Every morning his vallam returned with a huge catch along with the other vallams and launches that sailed ashore. Still, he wouldn't let her sleep. It infuriated him to see her sleep. Enfeebled by age, his frail body trembled with rage.

Inside the kitchen, muttering to herself, ammai was packing some gruel and dried fish curry in a small aluminium carrier for Cruz Michael who was going to sea. The curry was a little charred. It was Philomi who had cooked the dried fish that day.

No sooner Philomi entered the kitchen after washing her arms and feet by the well, than her ammai's voice grew strident. 'Etee… tawdry slut, what's this? You've charred the *karuvadu*. Which scoundrel of a fellow were you thinking of going around with, that you let the karuvadu burn? For all the measly work that your *Appan* does, he will jump up and down shouting that the karuvadu is all charred.'

On hearing her ammai's sharp words, Philomi who thought of going to Ranji's house stood leaning against the wall, her gaze fixed on the roof. Her chest convulsed with sobs.

Mariammai continued to bad mouth everyone. Cruz Michael went up to Siluvaiyadiyan's hut, called out loudly for him and returned home with him. Siluvai was his helper, who usually accompanied him on his vallam for the catch.

Siluvai had two children. His wife Innasi was an invalid. Mere skin and bones, she had been lying crippled and confined for several years in a dark corner of their small thatched hut. Even as her first child was born, she contracted tuberculosis. With that frail body of hers she bore Siluvai another child with great difficulty and somehow managed to bring it up. When she had gone to the hospital for the delivery of her second child, the doctor had warned her that she would die if she ever conceived again, and so Innasi didn't bear a child after that.

After Cruz Michael and Siluvai set out to sea, Mariammai got ready to go to the schoolmaster's house on the school street. When Mariammai came down the passageway, Philomi was standing by the pillar adjoining the thinnai. Her eyes still brimmed with tears. Mariammai shut the gate and yelled out as she walked, 'Ettee... don't go away somewhere leaving the house open. I'll go up to our schoolmaster's house and be back in a while. It seems his ammai is not well.'

Philomi didn't reply. She stood there letting her thoughts wander. Just now the boats would line the shore, all rigged and ready for the sail. As usual, the launches of Isaac, Rosario, Samidas' appachi and Uvariyur Ambrose would cruise headlong, riding the tumultuous waves at a full canter. Cruz Michael's vallam would set out last, trotting slowly. There was only Siluvai to push the vallam out into the sea. On days when the waves were high, at least two hands were needed just to push the vallam out into the sea. Earlier, when Philomi's thatha Dasaiyya had been alive, he would arrive promptly to help push the vallam, his lungi hitched up and tucked at his back. He would stagger as he fought with the waves. And Cruz Michael always shouted at him, 'Why do you have to do all this? What if you fall, eh? Move aside, I say… just move aside.'

'Elei, Cruz, you must be blessed to fall here and die… on Kadal Ammai's lap,' Dasaiyya would reply.

Philomi kutty herself had helped push the vallam out to sea on several occasions, her skirt drenched up to her waist even as she struggled with the waves. As for the other vallams, someone or the other at the seafront lent a helping hand. But none in the village came forward to push Cruz Michael's vallam. No one in the village liked Cruz Michael. He refused to pay his share of the tithe money for the church festivals. This feeling of resentment and animosity had been brewing for quite some time. No one had turned up even for Dasaiyya's burial. Only the pastor had come home to pray, defying the village. Sebasti, Cruz Michael, Amalorpavam akka's husband and Siluvaiyadiyan had carried the coffin to the churchyard. Isaac, however, had been of much help. He had gone to the churchyard ahead of them and dug a grave. Eventually, just one man from the village, Lasarup Paatta, had come for the burial. Lasarup Paatta was a dear old man. He loved everyone without disparity. And so he had turned up.

That day, Philomi had cried more than anyone else. Her ammai had kept carping and cavilling at all their relations. Whenever their kith and kin gathered at home for good or bad, she hollered as if she was about to be plundered. Every year Philomi's akka, Amalorpava Mary, came down for Christmas with her husband and children. So did Sebasti, his wife and children. On such occasions, a scrap was bound to rise for some petty reason or the other. It invariably festered into an ugly brawl and all of them left for their villages in a huff, vowing never to set foot on the doorstep of that house. And they promptly returned for the next Christmas.

As long as Dasaiyya had been alive, Mariammai had made it her habit to rail at him, calling him, 'a homeless old wretch' and a 'worthless scrounger.' She cursed loud enough for Cruz Michael's ears but he silenced her only once in a while. On the one hand, Cruz hated her with all his heart. Just the same, he feared her for no reason at all. Philomi never understood the why and wherefore of it all. Not a single day did Mariammai go to the seashore to await his vallam. Nor did she ever carry the basket bearing the day's catch. All she did was cook for them. Nonetheless, she wielded her authority over everyone in the house. Dasaiyya used to remark, 'Ettee… Philomi kutty, know what? Your ammai is a strange sea creature.' And Philomi would burst out laughing every time. Dasaiyya laughed too. Grandfather and granddaughter would laugh heartily, drowning the very roar of the waves. Only Philomi had wept and wailed inconsolably when Dasaiyya had died. Among those in that house, only she carried so many of his memories; enough to grieve endlessly over that old man's demise.

Seeing a shadow flitting close by, she looked up, startled. Samidas stood there with a smile, revealing his shiny white teeth. Unable to get over her surprise at seeing him there so suddenly, she stood staring at him in wide-eyed wonder.

'What is it Philomi kutty! You stare at me as if you would swallow me with your eyes!' he said, as he got on the thinnai.

'Who… is it you, really? When did you come? Have you been standing here for long? I didn't notice… was lost in thought. Come in.' She went in, rolled out a mat that stood against the wall, and asked him to sit. He continued to stand at the doorstep, holding the door frame, watching her spread the mat. Philomi lowered her head bashfully.

'Ammai has gone out,' she said.

'I know. I came here only after I saw your ammai leave,' he said as he came up to the mat and sat on his haunches, rolling up his lungi.

'You too sit, Philomi.'

Philomi sat near him on the mat. He pulled her closer to him by her shoulders and clasped her in a tight embrace. Philomi was frightened. What if her ammai were to come now? There could be nothing worse than that.

'No, no. If ammai comes back early, we are in for trouble.'

'Once she stirs out of the house, she doesn't return all that soon. I wanted to see you so badly that I didn't even go for the catch today.'

Philomi buried her face in his shoulder. He wore a half-sleeved, red vest. The taut muscles of his arms stood out beneath his rolled up sleeves. Philomi pulled his sleeves down and then rolled them up playfully. She tugged at the hair on his chest above the round collar of his vest.

'Sss... sss... what are you doing? It hurts.'

Philomi closed her mouth and laughed quietly. Nevertheless, she trembled inside. 'Here, ammai will be back now,' she thought fearfully. At the same time, she also mused along these lines, 'Let ammai come and see for herself. What can she do? She'll probably raise a ruckus, summoning the entire village. She'll tell appachi when he comes home. An enraged appachi will jump up and down. If Sebasti comes to know of it, he'll only stand by her. He knows that Samidas is a good paravan. Her sister

Amalorpavam wouldn't say anything either. Spurning the disapproval of his ammai and appachi, Sebastian will stick up for his sister. After all, he too had loved a girl – Ranji – once. Then everything will end well.'

Samidas got up to shut the door. He drew the bolt, and came back. Philomi looked at him in confusion. He laid his head on her lap. Philomi was at once terrified and happy. Samidas sensed her thighs tremble in fear.

'You frightened thing. Why are your thighs trembling so?' he said, laughing.

'Never mind that, do you know how I've been searching for you these two days? Where were you?'

'Did you come to my house?'

'No...'

'You should've come straight to my house and asked my appachi. You should've asked, 'Where's your son? I must talk to him.' Saying this, he broke into a loud guffaw. She fell about laughing as well, her face brushing his face on her lap.

'What did you eat today? Dried fish curry?' he asked.

'Yes… but how did you find out?' she asked amazed.

'Pooh… is that a big deal? Your laughter smells of dried fish.'

Samidas pushed her down on the mat suddenly. The end of her sari fell away. Her laughter hadn't subsided yet.

'No Sami… ammai will be back any minute. No… let me go. Why do you clasp me so hard?' she protested, her voice barely a whisper. He tormented her as he wished. Philomi neither resisted nor surrendered. She was both willing and unwilling. For a second, her ammai's scowling face appeared before her eyes. Then she forgot even that. By then, Samidas had possessed her completely. After that, Philomi was left with no words.

He got up. The first thing Philomi heard as soon as he disengaged himself from her, was the roar of the sea. Its deep rumble now sounded very close. It seemed to her as if the waves had rolled across the shore, swept past the coconut grove, the well and the backyard, and were rushing towards her. In a little while, those waves would carry her away and withdraw into the sea.

He had rolled up Philomi's sari and flung it in a corner. It lay near the wicker baskets. Not even conscious that she should wear it, she lay curled on the mat, her hands between her legs. Bathed in perspiration and fear, her body trembled. Samidas crouched gently behind her and craned forward to see her face. Philomi lifted her head slightly and looked at him. He too appeared confused. The silver cross on the chain he wore around his neck dangled out of his vest.

'Philomi, are you angry with me?'

She didn't reply. Her ears were tuned to the sea's deep rumble, its deafening roar.

'Mm? Are you angry with me? If it was wrong, will you forgive me?'

Philomi turned around and hugged him close to her waist.

'Sami, why did you have to come here now? Look what you've done now… coming here when ammai is away.'

Samidas couldn't even comfort her. He was full of

self-reproach. 'Chei… how disgraceful of me! How could I conduct myself in such a shameful way within a few moments? What will this poor Philomi kutty think of me? Was it merely for this that I thought she was mine all these years? Is this all then – my love for her?' he thought.

'Sami, you're still the same. Do you remember? When we were going to school together, we were playing behind the church one morning. You behaved just the same that day too, hugging me roughly and nuzzling me, remember?'

He kept staring at the coconut groves through the window.

Philomi got up and went to the backyard to wash herself. When she came back, the mat was empty. The front door and the bamboo gate lay wide open. She took the sari that lay near the wicker baskets and wrapping it hastily around herself, ran out into the street. At a distance, she saw Samidas walking away with lowered head. She stood there for a while, looking at him.

4

In the morning, as soon as she woke up, Philomi washed her face and started for the seashore. As usual, ammai lay sleeping in the hall, her limbs spread-eagled like a man. Philomi hadn't slept the previous night. Her eyes burnt. Her body ached. She closed the door, opened the fence gate and walked out into the street. When she stepped on the sandy street, it was all damp and chilly. The entire street that stretched along the seashore lay drenched in the dew that had fallen all night long. The tiled roofs, wet with dew, glistened and looked a bright red. Nothing was visible beyond seven or eight yards. Mist hung in a thick curtain everywhere.

It was impossible to stand on the seashore. The wind blew fiercely. As the sea lay hazy and indistinct, it was difficult to see anything approaching the shore. The place lay swaddled in a thick mist. In the coconut groves, the fronds rasped against one another in the wind, sounding like the laughter of a big, burly man.

When Philomi reached the shore, she found Isaac's wife Catherine already standing there, coughing. Two or three other women and a few children were faintly visible at a distance. Everyone – the women and children from all the streets of the parakudi – would be waiting there. The mist wrapped and enfolded them all. Though it was long since daybreak, there was no sign of the sun yet. Philomi went and stood by Catherine.

Clutching her stomach, Catherine coughed violently, the noise rising above the din of the sea. Unable to stand after that nasty fit of cough, she threw her fish basket upside down on the sand and sat on it.

'Akka, must you come to the seashore in this mist? Where's the big need to carry fish like this? We've been carrying fish ever since we were born, but our troubles don't seem to have come to an end. Must you carry them in this damp and chill, torturing yourself this way?' Philomi asked Catherine.

'I'll need some fish, anyway, to be salted and dried for karuvadu, won't I? Am I a blessed woman whose womb opened to bear a son I can send out to sea?' Catherine was once again racked by a violent fit of cough.

Philomi suddenly recalled what had happened the previous day but somehow, she couldn't bring herself to hate Samidas completely. They were now bound together, inseparably, she felt.

Far away, in the sea, the sails of the vallams grew distinct like the wings of white birds bobbing on water. Now the mist was dispersing at the sight of the sun. It was dissolving in thick mottled patches, as if someone had stirred it with a stick. Two or three motor launches were nearing the shore.

Catherine stood staring at those launches.

Isaac's launch came first, cruising headlong. The loud clatter of its engine ripped through the roar of the sea. Closely behind, rode the *Sea Bird*. It belonged to Samidas' father. It had been the first launch to arrive at the village. Isaac had named his launch *Catherine*. He had bought it when he and Catherine had been newly-married, and he had been very fond of her. On the day he bought the launch, he and Catherine rode out some distance into the sea on it. Standing on the edge of the launch, Catherine had laughed and waved happily to the villagers who stood watching on the shore. It was all an old story now. Catherine herself had forgotten all that. Once in a while, she wept recalling those days. The rest of the time she either coughed or put up with Isaac's beatings and abuses. This was her life now.

Isaac's launch laid anchor by the west end of the shore. It didn't come up to its usual place. So, Catherine ran along the shore where the surf crashed on the sand. She stumbled on a rock buried in the sand and fell down. The parava women, who stood at a distance, burst out laughing. Philomi flung her basket on the sand and ran to lift her up. By then a big wave rolled ashore and retreated, leaving Catherine completely drenched. Philomi lifted her up. Tossed by the waves, Catherine's basket drifted into the water. Philomi waded into the water and caught hold of it. Standing on the edge of his launch, Isaac waved his hands furiously and shouted at Catherine.

'Ei, you wanton whore, why don't you simply die? Must you come to the seashore instead? Aren't you ashamed?

Will any parachi fall down like this, making a spectacle of herself in front of these sniggering wretches? Hurry up, you worthless creature!'

Catherine took the basket from Philomi. She could only limp as she had hurt her knee. 'Akka walk slowly. What's the big hurry? Don't mind him. He always yells like that. Walk slowly, akka,' said Philomi.

Philomi came back to the place where her basket lay. The parachis standing around couldn't suppress their sniggers and giggles as yet. Rosario Fernandes' eldest daughter-in-law, Supi, looked at those around her meaningfully and said in mocking tones, 'Don't you sinners have even a drop of the human feeling and compassion that this Philomi kutty has?

'Oh come, come, even you were gawking at the boats, looking to see which fellow was coming ashore. Feeling sorry that a sickly woman had fallen down, this kutty rushed to lift her up,' retorted one of them.

'Why should I lift her up? Won't I catch her sickness then? After all, she's Philomi kutty's akka in a way. Isn't this kutty going to marry Isaac and go to his house, sooner or later? Look how affectionate she already is towards her co-wife,' Supi said, her eyes wide-open in mock amazement.

Philomi burned to give her a fitting reply. But she stood silent, her gaze fixed on the vallams approaching at a distance. Tears stung her eyes.

By then, the seashore was swarming with fishmongers and trading agents. Little children, with nothing around their waists, were picking shells. Noah's eight-year-old daughter Christie ran around naked, gathering shells. Those children always looked bigger for their age. They were the loved ones of Kadal Ammai. Any child born at the sea front, no matter how wealthy the family is, never suckles at its mother's breast first. As soon as a child is born, the family pours a bit of the salty sea water into its mouth. This water endows boys with the courage to battle the fierce winds and tumultuous waves; it gives girls the grit to bear stoically the disappointments and sorrows they may encounter in their lives. From time immemorial, their lives are inextricably bound with the sea. They hold Kadal Ammai on par with Yesu and Marial and worship her with equal reverence. In return, she showers them with fish from her large womb. There has never been any unity among them. And their morals aren't straight either. So many incidents, so many happenings. Kadal Ammai bears everything patiently because she loves her children dearly. Didn't this Philomi sleep with Samidas yesterday? The sea didn't snatch her life away for that reason. The sea is pure, sacred whereas their hutments are dirty and squalid.

The vallams, country boats and launches reached the shore. The seafront stirred alive, bustling with activity. Fishmongers, trading agents and money lenders thronged the seafront, their noisy hustle and loud cries rising above the roar of the waves. The children were picking the fish that fell off the boats when the nets were gathered and the day's catch was hauled ashore. Rosario Fernandez smacked Timothy's son on his back for having picked cast-off fish from his launch. Sobbing pitifully, the little boy ran away in search of his father. Poor child, his mother had died two years back.

As it was the day before the full moon, the tide was high and the waves strong. The catch was smaller than usual. Nevertheless, the launch owners had managed a big haul as always. If the sea was choppy and the waves by Siluvai Parai – a cluster of rocks mid-sea – were unruly, it was impossible for the small vallams and other country boats to venture as far out as that. Besides, there were any number of small whirlpools out there. Once you crossed to the far side of Siluvai Parai, the sea lay placid like a pond. This particular place was Kadal Ammai's treasure trove. If the vallams ever went there on days when the waves were high, they would be simply sucked in by the eddies. The launches somehow made it always, braving the wind and the waves, no matter how fierce they were. That day too, the launches had steered beyond Siluvai Parai and cast their nets. The vallams and boats, however, had simply stood on this side. Not everyone could afford a launch. The launches turned out to be a fierce rival among them. Ever since their arrival, there had been bitter strife between them and the vallams, over and above the roar of the deep. As a result, the village lay divided. An ugly wart appeared on their quiet, unobtrusive lives which had hitherto progressed peacefully. The small country boats and vallams couldn't compete with the big launches. The days when they set out into the restless sea, singing in unison, were now a thing of the past. It would no longer be a surprise if in an ugly brawl, a vallam owner stabbed a launch owner. To that extent had vengeance sprung forth its shoots within them.

The impoverished vallam and other country boat owners borrowed heavily from the Kulasekara Pattinam Sayibus. They never managed to pay off those debts. They ended up borrowing again and again. On days when the sea was lashed by fierce winds and rain, making it impossible for them to go fishing, the Sayibus gave them money after making them sign on revenue stamps affixed to blank sheets of paper. In lieu of the interest money, they came to the seashore every day and took away the fish at a price they fixed. The Sayibus bought the fish at half or sometimes even a quarter of the rates offered by regular fishmongers and traders. But none questioned all that. They knew very well that if they dared to raise the matter, they wouldn't get any credit the next time they needed it.

The cloth sail that propelled Cruz Michael's vallam in the direction of the wind was torn and patched in several places. Notwithstanding that, he kept it. It was this self-same sail that he unfurled against the wind at sea.

Alex who had come from Pazhaya Kaayal village had a new vallam and a new sail cloth – a pale pink in colour, the delicate shade of roses. What's more, he had named his vallam *Pattu Rosa* - silken rose. Siluvai fancied quitting Cruz Michael's old, rickety vallam and becoming an oarsman in Alex's new one, but somehow, he couldn't break away from Cruz Michael. Day after day, when they returned from the sea, he thought of telling Cruz Michael, '*Muthalali*, I wish to quit. You must please allow this Siluvai to leave,' but couldn't bring himself to do it. Several days and months passed this way. Siluvai was still unable to go over to another vallam.

Carrying her basket, Philomi walked towards the vallam. Siluvai was fixing the oar with a rope.

'You mustn't say that. The catch is awfully small today. It is by Marial's grace that we sailed through the winds and returned ashore…'

Not paying heed to any of the usual haggling over the price of fish that went on around her, Philomi stood looking far out into the sea where a vallam was returning ashore tardily. Rocked by the waves, it tottered ashore all alone. The sight of it wrenched her heart. She did not know whose vallam it was. Suddenly, for no reason, she remembered Samidas' pale face. Philomi shuddered.

When it came to bandying words, you could never get the better of the Tharaganaar, the agent who bought and sold fish wholesale. Though Cruz Michael always pleaded hoarsely with him for a better price for his fish, he eventually gave them away for the price set by the Tharaganaar. This was not without reason, though. The Tharaganaar had done so much for Cruz's family. As he handed over the fish to him, Cruz said, 'All is lost… Ever since the launches arrived at these shores, the vallams lost their livelihood and the paravan his peace of mind.' He looked with intense loathing at the launches which stood some distance away. The haggling over the price of the fish hadn't still come to an end there.

'Elei, how can you say that with such certainty, son? Won't you buy a launch someday too? How much longer can you put to sea on your appachi's vallam? Even if you don't manage to buy one, your grandson- this wretch Philomi's son – will set out to sea only on a launch. My grandson will be his agent then. Aren't the times changing?' the Tharaganaar said laughing and looked at Philomi. Philomi was casting the fish meant to be salted and sun-dried into her basket. There was a predominance of pomfret in the catch that day.

'Oh, yes… as if a groom is waiting for her at the doorstep just now! Why talk idly?'

'Etee… Philomi, what's this? Heard what your appachi is saying?' The Tharaganaar winked at her.

Philomi was busy picking the fish. The end of her sari had slipped off her shoulder and lay soaking on the wet sand. The swell of her dark, fulsome breasts and the sight of her white bodice sticking out of her blouse enraged Siluvai who stood watching from the vallam.

'Come on now *mama*, even if a girl were to marry and settle down, can she hope to live peacefully at this seafront? Only when the struggles at sea abate, will a parachi's troubles come to an end. Marriage is the only thing I lack now,' Philomi retorted.

'Look at the way she speaks. Etee… why were you born in this parakudi? Were you in my house, would I let you suffer like this?'

'What can be done, mama? A girl must go through what she is destined to. All the same, mama, you're so full of desire improper for your age.' Forgetting herself, Philomi laughed. The Tharaganaar laughed heartily too. Cruz and Siluvai were hauling the boat ashore. Whenever the Tharaganaar and Philomi fell talking, time passed gaily, filled with laughter and light-hearted banter. After she had finished picking the fish, Philomi gathered the end of her sari and flung it casually over her shoulder. 'Etee… why is neckline of your blouse so low? Even this decrepit old man feels desirous. Isn't it enough that this seafront is crawling with vile, loathsome men? Must you go about like this too, forgetting yourself?' the Tharaganaar chided her.

'Oh… it was only for your eyes, Mama,' Philomi retorted gaily. 'Which other fellow dares to gawk at this Philomi? Besides, is it something new? Doesn't every woman look the same? The womenfolk in the houses of these men, they have it too, don't they? You mustn't cast such stealthy glances when I'm not looking, else, I'll report it to *Mami…*' said Philomi as she walked away.

'Mischievous parachi!' said the Tharaganaar raising his hand, as if to strike her.

***

When Philomi walked home, her heart felt light. Chatting with the Tharaganaar mama always felt so good; this life and all the hardships in it seemed light and insubstantial and you grew hopeful. She liked him as much as she liked her beloved Ranji. These people had some strange charm about them. With it, they were able to make everyone happy. Not everyone possessed it, though. Her ammai – how sorely she lacked it!

After speaking to the Tharaganaar, even Samidas'

behaviour the previous day no longer affected her deeply. In fact, she hadn't spoken to the Tharaganaar about it. It had been the usual chinwagging about mundane things. But somehow, her heart felt light as if she had talked it all out with him. Nonetheless, she must be careful from now on. She thought she must keep track of her monthly periods. She couldn't bring herself to hate Samidas even now. On the contrary, she loved him wholeheartedly now. Were Samidas to become hers, she would lack for nothing in this world. At once, she said the Lord's prayer within her heart. She felt as if she and Samidas were already away in a brave new world peopled by genial folk like Ranji and Tharaganaar mama who only spread joy around them. Feeling buoyant and carefree, she opened the gate of the bamboo fence and entered the house.

5

There was still a month left for Christmas. Making preparations for the festival was something that Mariammai loved doing. Around this time of the year, she was usually lively and high spirited. So much so, she even forgot to scold Philomi. This year, akka and annan had written that they would be coming home.

Akka did not write often but when a letter did arrive from her, Philomi never tired of reading it over and over again. The letter had come in a blue cover. She read it many times over that day. Still, she couldn't get enough of it. Akka had written at length about Philomi and her marriage plans for her.

That year too, as usual, the mist came down heavily just before the festival. As a matter of fact, it was the mist, wasn't it, which brought the festival? Philomi's heart brimmed over on hearing the peal of the church bells reverberating through the mist for the morning service. She felt as if the sound came floating down from the distant heaven. The month of December always wove a magic spell. At dawn, the children who practised for the Christmas carol service began setting out in flocks. Though she had vivid recollections of the festival ever since she could remember, it seemed new each year. That year, it was decided that they should all go to Vepangattur to buy clothes for the festival. Udankudi was barely a mile from Vepangattur. Mariammai could even get to watch a nice movie there.

Samidas came over again on a day when her ammai was away. He took her to the Tharaganaar's grove behind the church. He spoke as if he had completely forgotten what had happened the other day. She too didn't find it agreeable to talk about it all over again. She wished her ammai would come just then and see her walking with him. She longed to go away and live with him. But her ammai never came. That day too she had gone to the schoolmaster's house. When she was with the schoolmaster, ammai never noticed time passing. The schoolmaster and ammai belonged to the same village – Punnaikaayal.

Samidas' marriage was more or less settled. The bride was from Uvariyur. He disclosed this piece of news to her at the grove and watched her. For a long time, Philomi remained still, her eyes shut, listening to the roar of the sea. At last, tears welled up in her eyes.

'Now what are you crying for?'

'Isn't the parachi born to cry? I feel like crying, I'm crying...' she said quietly.

'You think I'd forsake you and marry that girl from Uvariyur, isn't that so?'

'No… I don't think so…'

'Then why are you crying?'

She didn't reply. They stood quietly, lost in their own thoughts. After sometime, Philomi spoke, her eyes rivetted on the Tharaganaar's thoroughbred hens scratching about in the grove some distance away. 'Sami, nothing happens as we wish. It's getting late. Ammai will search for me. Appachi will be getting ready for the sea. You must go too, mustn't you? Get up.' She tugged at his hands. Like a child who implicitly obeyed her words, he rose and followed her. When they had set out in the evening, they had walked together, side by side. He couldn't bring himself to say anything to her now. Like a perceptive woman, she had persuaded him to get up and was now walking ahead of him, in complete control of herself. Seeing him plodding behind, deep in thought, she asked, 'Why do you walk with lowered head… mm? Is it something you can't even tell your Philomi?'

'Nothing…'

'You asked me why I was upset just now. What are you worrying about then? I've complete trust in you. You don't doubt me either. What if years fly by? Who can forget how we loved each other? Look at this Ranji. Did she forget my brother Sebasti even after she married and left? Or for that matter did he forget her? Why, the whole world goes on like this. I'm not feeling sad about anything. It is enough if you come to our gate and call out for me. This Philomi will come running to you. Even if you don't, she'll live happily, carrying your memories. That's all there is to it. The Lord must will everything. Let me go. Be happy.' Saying this, she walked through the backyard of her house not even turning to look at his face.

Samidas stood watching till she disappeared from sight and then headed towards the toddy shop.

Having consoled him so bravely, she came and sat on the parapet of the well, torn by grief. She was convulsed with tears.

She looked back longingly at the days when as a child she had happily roamed the seaside with her thatha, picking conches and seashells.

Hearing her appachi call her from the front door, she wiped her tears and went in.

***

Ranji stopped by that evening. She had come to tell Philomi that she was leaving for her husband's village. She went and sat by the well, her usual haunt every time she came to Philomi's house.

What a wonderful thing frienship is! What does age have to do with it? Philomi placed her head indulgently on Ranji's lap and lay down. Their conversation was tinged with sorrow; with the sadness that comes from parting; with joy; and also with the anguish of those who meet after a long absence. If only she could lie like that forever, her head on Ranji's lap. Why did Ranji have to get married? Must she get married too and go away someday?

She told her about Samidas. Ranji bent down, bringing her face very close to Philomi's and listened. Then she sighed deeply and said, 'You find all this new. I'm used to such things. Don't you know how deeply I loved your annan? A woman is born to weep in this world. And if the parachi begins to weep, this very sea will go dry. I'm amused by it all now. Philomi, this feeling of affection, love – it's all an illusion. Look at me now… I'm unable to return my husband's affection for me. It seems to me that we can love only one person with all our heart in our life. I'm no longer so deeply attached to anyone. That annan of yours made off with all the love in my heart. You'll perhaps find all this new. Must stifle it all within your heart, Philomi. After all, how long are we going to live, tell me? Don't let your mind wander.'

Philomi kept quiet. They remained quiet for a long time, savouring the silence. In truth, their wordlessness was very eloquent at that moment.

It was finally Ranji who broke it.

'Philomi, shall I leave then? I hope to come for the festival. But every time I come here, I'm unable to stay for more than a couple of days. That husband of mine – he's totally helpless without me; can't manage a thing by himself... that's how he is. Don't break your head over anything. You'll forget it all soon; true, it'll be a great torture till you forget it all. But you'll get over it. Be happy. Will stop by if I come for the festival. Shall I leave then?'

Philomi walked up to the street with Ranji. She stood watching her tearfully till she turned into her street. What a lofty place Ranji occupied in her heart! Philomi was proud to think of her.

When she entered the house, though, her heart felt bereft.

She couldn't put everything out of her mind and deceive herself, as simply and easily as Ranji had made it out to be. The next morning, she didn't get up to go out to the seafront. Mariammai usually woke up very late. Even the sun had entered the house through the back door that day. Only after she was struck by the sun's rays did Mariammai stir from her deep slumber. By then Cruz and Siluvai had returned from the sea. Though Mariammai kept grumbling that Philomi hadn't gone to the seashore that day, Philomi heard nothing except the ceaseless roar of the sea. Her body burnt like fire.

For nearly four or five days, Philomi lay bedridden, not wanting to eat, not wanting to do anything. Meanwhile, the Tharaganaar came all the way to their home one day to see her. He chided her ammai and appachi severely. Philomi's lips were chapped. Not having seen a drop of oil for days, her hair was dishevelled. She lay weak and emaciated. The Tharaganaar went home and sent a bottle of medicine though his servant.

Cruz Michael grew very quiet, though he continued to go out to drink toddy in the evenings with Isaac. When he returned home drunk, he came and sat by Philomi's bed and kept staring vacantly at her. Among his children, he was most fond of her. His love was as vast as his dear sea; and as deep, but never did he exhibit it. Even now he did nothing but simply sit next to her, looking at her wasted form. Such was his love. For two days he didn't put to sea. As if going out and drinking with Isaac was not enough, he also swilled some toddy from time to time all by himself.

Once drunk, he simply sat beside Philomi. Nothing of this affected Mariammai in the least. She continued to spend all her evenings at the schoolmaster's house. When Mariammai returned home very late one night, Cruz Michael vented out all the anger he had hitherto supressed by thrashing her soundly. Mariammai took off to Isaac's house that night, stayed there a long time, weeping, and eventually fell asleep.

The medicine sent by the Tharaganaar did nothing to bring down the fever. Only after a senior doctor from Kulasekara Pattinam came and examined her, nearly a week later, did they come to know that it was typhoid.

In the meantime, one Sunday, Sebasti came down to see her. Amalorpavam akka was unable to come. Instead, she wrote a letter. They were soon hard up, struggling to even scrape together their daily meal, leave alone meet the medical expenses. As Cruz stopped going to sea, Siluvai rode the vallam alone but he kept close to the shore. The catch he brought ashore was very poor. The Tharaganaar refused to take the fish due to him. Instead, he bought off the fish at a rate, handed the money to Siluvai and asked him to give it to Cruz. The Tharaganaar had a very kind heart, to say nothing of the special affection he had for Philomi.

Once it became known that it was typhoid fever, even Mariammai forgot her evening pleasures and started staying at home. Motherly love sprang forth even in her heart. She fetched the pastor herself one day and requested him to hold a prayer service. One evening, when Cruz had gone out, her beloved schoolmaster came home. He sat close to Philomi, took both her hands and held them lovingly on his lap. Philomi could barely open her eyes and see him. Nevertheless, she could feel the depth of his affection in his hands. Mariammai remained looking at his face. Then she made some coffee for him. Without exchanging a single word, they were all making known their love and fondness for one another. Philomi wished she could die at that moment.

***

Philomi grew thin as a reed. Her once rounded cheeks were now sunken. Her blouses hung loosely around her body. The typhoid fever had not just changed her looks, it had transformed her heart too. A mature, wise woman who had learnt to observe everything with detachment was born within her. Lying in bed, she kept mulling over things, not knowing how else to pass time. She thought a lot about her life, of times gone by and the people around her. A strange clarity emerged within her. When she wasn't thinking about anything, she simply listened to the roar of the sea. It brought such tranquillity to her heart. On the whole, the fever had done her good. She was finally able to accept life as it was. The poor girl had even more or less begun to forget Samidas. She somehow understood that there was no room for pointless feelings in real life. How happy Ranji would feel if she told her all this.

Two days before the festival, Sebasti came down from Vepangattur with his family and so did akka Amalorpavam Mary. In her heart of hearts, Mariammai did feel a little sad that she had not been able to go to Udankudiyur to buy clothes that year. Upon her recovery, Philomi had a proper bath only the day before the festival. It was Amalorpavam who helped her bathe, as she was still weak. Philomi revelled in her sister's love as Amalorpavam gently poured the water prepared carefully with turmeric and neem leaves over her head. Even the Tharaganaar came home that day. He was beside himself with joy that Philomi had finally recovered. He had prayed for Philomi and had undertaken to fulfil a vow at the mosque by the river bank on her recovery. 'What's in our hands? Allah must will everything,' he said as he took leave of them. Cruz Michael didn't forget to invite him for the festival too. Though he had borrowed heavily for Philomi's sake, he felt very happy.

Sebasti and Amalorpavam had tried to outdo each other in buying clothes for the festival. Only Philomi looked weak and thin. Sebasti's two little brats were happily engrossed in making stars and lanterns out of bamboo splits. Philomi had no work. Admiring the handiwork of her two little nephews, she rendered them what little help she could every now and then. Amalorpavam akka's little girl Mary climbed on to her thin, emaciated lap and fell asleep. The beauty and grace of certain moments in life cannot be described in words. They can only be experienced. Philomi felt very happy. Though life was not spread all the way with happiness, she was now willing to believe that it was indeed a joyful affair.

Sebasti had a lot of work that day. Having gone to the shop to buy things for making sweets and other eatables for the festival, he and Amalorpavam's husband returned home well past noon. His two little boys had stubbornly tagged along with them. His wife lay on a mat in the hall, reading a book. She was not used to doing any work away from her home town.

After her recovery from the typhoid fever, Philomi glowed with an inexplicable beauty. It was the kind of strange, serene radiance that hangs about you after a terrible bout of fever. Confined to the house all these days, she now came out and sat on the thinnai, watching the street and the houses on the opposite row as if they were all strange and unfamiliar. She slowly walked up to the street and looked on either side. The village had changed a lot, or so it appeared to her. That impression surprised her and filled her with a newfound joy. She couldn't fathom the why or wherefore of it all, yet she cherished it.

As usual, Isaac's voice thundered loudly from his house.

That night Cruz's house reverberated with untold happiness. About evening, Siluvai came and hung a star lantern stuck with colourful bits of paper on the *karuvai* tree in front of the house. The light from the paper lantern scattered on all four sides and cast its radiant hue everywhere. A tiny speck of that light fell as far as the hall. Cruz Michael had drunk in moderation that day. None of the adults slept that night. They kept awake to attend the midnight mass. The womenfolk were busy until then. Sebasti and Amalorpavam's husband stretched themselves out by the window in the hall. They looked so tranquil in their sleep, bringing to mind the beatific faces of men who slept soundly after a hard day's toil. A big *jamukkalam* had been spread out on the floor and the children made to sleep on that. As little Mercy was in the habit of wetting her bed, they had put her down in a corner, away from the rest. After Sebasti chided her, his wife joined Mariammai and Amalorpavam, assisting them in their chores. They didn't allow Philomi to do any work, though.

The mist always arrives hand in hand with Christmas. In fact, it is this mist which lends a special beauty to Christmas. Walking through the mist to attend the Christmas service and the peal of the church bells reverberating through the mist- how utterly lovely these are.

The school boys and teachers who were part of the carol service came singing the story of Christ. Senior teacher Samuel Jebaraj's voice soared above the rest. Walking ahead of them all, was a small boy holding aloft a petromax light. He was Rosario's grandson. For some days now, Rosario had been going around bragging to all and sundry in the village that his grandson was to sing in the carols. It turned out that the poor boy had to sing and carry the petromax light as well. A big task indeed for such a mite of a fellow.

On hearing the carollers, Philomi ran out to the street, only to rush back into the house to wake up the little ones. Only half awake, they rubbed their eyes sleepily and followed her.

Cruz Michael chided Philomi. 'Why do you wake up the little ones in this mist and cold? As if they have never seen carol singing in their villages.'

Sebasti's eldest son proudly pointed out the star lantern on the karuvai tree to the other children. After the carollers went past their house, none of the children went back to sleep. They sat huddled around Philomi in the faint light that fell on the thinnai, listening to the film stories she told them.

At half past eleven, they set out for the midnight mass. The church had hired a radio from Kulasekara Pattinam for the occasion and the Christian hymns it played out were faintly audible. As they walked through the streets, a small scuffle broke out among the children as to who should hold Philomi's hands. Amalorpavam's husband scolded his children. Asir then reluctantly held his appachi's hand. Mercy wouldn't listen though. She insisted on holding Philomi's hand. Despite Cruz's entreaties that they should hold his hand, not one of the children listened. After a while, the grown-ups happily let them be. The pure and simple love of those little ones left Philomi speechless. Tears welled up in her eyes. If only she could spend the rest of her life with these children. Mariammai, Amalorpavam, Philomi and Sebasti's wife walked in front, while the men followed behind. As they neared Ranji's house, they spotted her standing near the thinnai, watching the street. As soon as Ranji saw them, she ran in hurriedly. In a while, she came out with her husband close behind. Philomi ran forward and hugged her. Ranji's husband joined Philomi's people.

6

That very same evening Amalorpavam left for her village with her husband and children. Sebasti and his family were to leave the next day.

As a rule, no one usually ventured out to sea on Christmas. The Tharaganaar, who had been invited for lunch, stayed chatting with them until evening, as if he were one of them. No matter whose house he went to, the Tharaganaar could so effortlessly mingle with the family, becoming one of them. He was a stranger to none.

Siluvai came and collected his gift of money, dhoti, towel and sweets. His little son had come along with him. The Tharaganaar gave him ten paise. More than the sweets he ate there, it was this little gift of money that delighted the child. Though Cruz was heavily drunk, he managed to keep steady. The Tharaganaar told him he would lend him some money for a launch. He also suggested that Cruz petition the Government for the remaining sum. Cruz was reluctant though and mulled over it. Selling his vallam in the event of buying a launch was simply out of the question. As to what would become of the vallam after his lifetime, he was not disposed to be anxious about it, presently. Still, he couldn't refute the Tharaganaar's words right away.

'Son, think over the matter and let me know. In any case, what's the big hurry now? Don't break your head over it all by yourself. Talk it over with Sebasti and your wife. I'm saying this only for your own good. Just remember that you have another girl to marry off… I'll get going then. The lorries are due for loading today…' said the Tharaganaar as he left.

Mariammai sneaked to the backyard, took a bottle of toddy from behind the parapet of the well, guzzled some of it and let out a loud belch. She wiped the toddy that had trickled down the corner of her mouth with the back of her palm. Philomi, who happened to come to the back door just then, looked at it with disgust and went back into the house. Mariammai crumpled the end of her sari into a small ball, held it over her mouth and walked in. She then rolled out a mat in the rear portion of the house and stretched down. Sebasti had gone to the seashore with his wife and children. Philomi longed to go somewhere too. Suddenly, her heart grew empty. Memories rushed in a torrent and Samidas encroached most of her thoughts. Couldn't she ever forget him?

Samidas' visit the other day when her ammai was away, his passionate lovemaking, how she had willingly or unwillingly given in to him, their conversation in the Tharaganaar's grove – she recalled everything in no particular order. She leaned against the wall and wept softly. 'Yesuve, let me forget everything…' she murmured.

She heard Siluvai's voice outside. He was arguing with Cruz. It shook her out of her sorrows.

'Muthalali, all the launch owners are setting out to sea. Isaac, Rosario, Uvariyur Ambrose, church street Rosario – they're all ready. The vallam owners are thinking of going as well. That's why I came... to fetch the net. Pavulu Paatta is standing there...'

'Elei... what's this new practice, eh? Who goes to sea on the Lord's birthday? These launch fellows are getting cheekier by the day. Go tell them that those who venture into the sea today won't return ashore. Wait... I'll come too. No need for the net. Fat louts... did they think it was the sea or the *Tiruchendur Kadamba* pond? If they go to sea today, which of them will return alive... eh? None of the parachis can hope save their *thaali*, they'll all be left weeping and wailing over their dead men. Di... Philomi, fetch that machete!'

Siluvai was gone. Cruz's eyes were red with fury and the tip of his dark nose quivered in rage. Without uttering a word, Philomi wiped her eyes, went in and took out the bill hook machete from between the stacked pots, trembling as she did so. As she handed it to Cruz, she said, 'Appachi, why get into all this fuss and furore?' Her voice betrayed her fears.

'What do you know? Those setting out on vallams haven't the means to make a decent haul but fattened up by money, these launch fellows have the nerve to go to sea even on Yesu's birthday. Perhaps, they think that we vallam fellows are worthless scum... you stay at home. I'll be back.'

He fastened the machete to the waist string he wore above his lungi and strode down the street, planting his feet wide apart. Stopping that paravan would be impossible now. Philomi sank on the thinnai as she watched him go. For a while, she was aware of nothing but the roar of the sea.

Suddenly, when she looked at the sky, she spotted a large flock of sea cormorants flying from right to left. The fisherfolk considered it a bad omen. Any paravan would think twice about stirring out of his house at such times. Philomi could feel her heart pounding. 'Yesu aiyya…' she murmured as she closed her eyes and leaned her head against the pillar of the thinnai.

Just then, Mariammai rose to go to the backyard. Still tipsy and groggy, she stumbled and fell on the stone threshold of the passageway. Her nose hit the sharp edge of the stone. Not a sound rose from her throat. Only a feeble moaning was faintly audible. Philomi didn't hear it at all. The blood that oozed from Mariammai's nose trickled down the stone threshold and lay congealed. How could she lie prone on the floor there, oblivious to everything, forgetting even her beloved schoolmaster?

Philomi's eyes were closed but her mind was restless, wide awake. She stood all alone on a rock in the middle of a vast, shoreless sea. She was in extravagant apparel – the Queen Sheeba's costume she had worn in a school play when she was in the fifth class. Huge waves rolled towards her and left her drenched up to her waist. Strewn under her feet were countless shells and conches she had run around and gathered as a child by the seashore.

7

When Cruz reached the seashore, it was in a great ferment. The air was split by the loud roar of the sea on one side and the noisy clamour of the paravars on the other. Isaac had climbed on to his launch and was speaking at the top of his voice with furious gesticulations so much so his lungi kept slipping from his waist.

Cruz walked up to Pavulu Paatta who stood in front of the crowd. 'Come, Cruz.' Paatta greeted him.

'What's happening here?'

'What will happen? It seems the launch owners are setting out to sea…'

'Pavulu Paatta, how old are you? Have you ever gone to sea on a festival day in your lifetime? Tell me?'

'No…'

'Why waste words then? Fetch your machete, let's see which launch fellow dares to enter the sea today. Elei… Timothy, Asir… why do you stand there watching? Let's show them there are a hundred and eight vallam owners in this village. Elei… Isaac, you were born to a parachi and so was I. When have we gone to sea on a festival day, eh? Why do you make such a ruckus standing on your launch? Get down, you scumbag.' Cruz hollered.

'*Vei*... Cruz, mind your words. The sea is not your wife's property. We'll set out and return as and when we please.' Isaac yelled angrily, over and above the roar of the sea.

'Try setting out on your launch and then you'll know. I'll set it on fire, mind you!'

'Fuck off, you swine! Just try doing that!' Isaac jumped from his launch into the knee-deep water and advanced menacingly towards Cruz. Samidas' father, Rosario and Ambrose followed suit, with their men close at heel. Pulling the machete out of his waist belt and brandishing it furiously, Cruz rushed forward. Some four or five vallam owners sprang up at once and restrained him.

Pavulu Paatta lambasted them all.

'Elei... murderous fellows, do you think this is your stinking parakudi? This is the sea, you scoundrels, the sea. You, son of the devil, how dare you brandish your machete?' he shoved Cruz aside angrily and snatching his machete, he flung it away on the sand. On hearing Pavulu Paatta's loud rebukes, Isaac, Rosario and the other launch owners stopped short and slunk away. Pavulu Paatta looked at the launch owners in disgust. His eyes misted over with tears. His wrinkled and weather-beaten body trembled. He looked at the launches bobbing up and down in the waves with loathing and turned towards the launch owners.

'Elei... have you bought these launches only to bring death and destruction to this parakudi? The paravan must never be greedy. A greedy paravan will never come to any good. Which seafront has seen men venturing into the sea on a festival day? Is this the sea or the ditch by your huts? Isn't this the sea that cleaved aside, making way for the child who came searching for his father who had gone fishing? Try venturing into the sea today... let's see if you have the guts. We'll simply go over to your houses and tell your women, your husbands won't return alive today. Go get into the sea!' he shouted furiously.

None of them spoke. Cruz stood staring at the sea. The launch owners didn't dare to enter the sea after that. They departed westward with their men. Pavulu Paatta turned to the vallam owners and said, 'What are you still hanging around for? They've all left, haven't they? Elei... Cruz, such unchecked anger is no good at all. Perhaps, you drank a lot today. What are you still hanging around here for? Come... come.' He gently steered the crowd away from the place.

Pavulu Paatta was the oldest among the paravars. He was a wizened old man and yet the courage to ride out to sea alone and cast his net single-handedly still glimmered in his heart. He was an exceptional man. No parava boy who set out to sea for the first time with his appachi forgot to take Pavulu Paatta's blessings. Often, when they needed to settle matters of dispute in the village, the paravars sought his counsel only. Their trust in him was complete, not unlike the faith they placed in Yesu. Though he had never set foot outside their parakudi, there was nothing he didn't know. He owned a vallam, a rickety old thing and it still rode the waves.

The crowd broke up and everyone dispersed into the village. Thanks to Pavulu Paatta, a heinous murder had been averted that day.

Siluvai, who walked along with Cruz, parted company halfway and headed towards his house. As soon as Cruz turned into his street, Isaac's wife Catherine came running towards him, her hair streaming loose.

'Oh, mama, Mariammai *athai* has left us all… mama.' Distraught with grief, she beat her chest and came running towards him despite her illness.

'Etee… what are you saying? Don't shock me to my death, you sinner! Tell me it isn't true…' Cruz caught hold of her hands and implored.

'It's true, mama… your wife fell on the stone threshold at your backdoor, broke her nose and died. Philomi kutty and Sebasti fell unconscious on seeing her. We had to sprinkle water on their faces to bring them around. I came searching for you.'

'My Yesu! Why did you inflict such terrible suffering upon my family?' He beat his chest and ran towards his house, wailing bitterly. Clutching his arm, Catherine went along with him.

***

Three days had passed since Mariammai died.

The launches and vallams went to sea as usual. The launch owners and vallam owners continued to squabble over fishing as always. Only Cruz was oblivious to everything. He didn't even recognize his near and dear ones. As long as she was alive, he detested Mariammai with all his heart as she kept visiting the schoolmaster. On occasion, he had even entered into a drunken fracas with the schoolmaster. But she couldn't bear not to see the schoolmaster. Initially, she frequented his house almost every day, but as years passed and she grew older, her visits to his house grew few and far between. However, on no account did she stop seeing him completely. So close was their friendship. She didn't relinquish her friendship in the hustle and bustle of marriage and child bearing. She kept visiting him through it all – when she bore Cruz's first child Amalorpavam, when she gave birth to Sebasti two years later and when Philomi was born several years after Sebasti. Cruz never understood her heart's desires to this day. Perhaps, her schoolmaster was wise to them.

Even now Cruz wouldn't willingly call her cruel. He had never been able to ignore her completely. True, he hated her. All the same, his desire for her knew no bounds for she had an allure of her own. She had a strong, shapely figure and just lying on her lap was enough to infuse a man with courage and prudence. She had never thought of betraying Cruz. She was truly a strange parachi.

Philomi's feeble body somehow endured her ammai's death, but Sebasti – how he wept like a child. The schoolmaster had come for the funeral too – not to their house but to the churchyard. He couldn't cry like the others. He stood watching the rites performed for her in vacant-eyed despair. Would he ever find a friend like her again? All in all, her death brought out in the open the affection people had for her. But Mariammai would never know. As long as she had been alive, she had believed that everyone except her schoolmaster despised her. How unfortunate! She died never realizing that so many harboured a deep love for her.

Cruz hadn't eaten a morsel since her death. The Tharaganaar stopped by from time to time and comforted him as much as he could. But who could fathom the anguish and yearning in that paravan's heart?

Cruz sat all the time on the string cot in the thinnai. He didn't know how the long nights of the cold season passed. He simply stared at the alternating daylight and darkness. Like a child, he sat gazing at the sky all day. Even the sight of the sea cormorants, winging back to their nests in large flocks after foraging the sea for food, didn't bring his dear sea to his mind. The day after the sixteenth day rites, Sebasti prepared to leave for his village.

'Appachi… all rites are over. Two other teachers in my wife's school have gone on leave as well, so she won't get any more leave. The children too have been missing school… so, I'm leaving today.'

'Mm…'

'If you are going to sit forlorn like this, how can things be kept going? Only if you set out to sea, will there be fire in the oven. We had to borrow money as it is for ammai's funeral…'

'Mm…'

'Akka has left too and I'm leaving today as well. Don't let this Philomi kutty starve. Poor thing, she knows nothing. Must find a groom for her as soon as possible and get her married.'

'Mm...'

'I've already told you and the Sayibu has been asking me too. If you wash your hands off all this and come over there, we can put up a shop and get this girl married. You needn't rove the sea any longer at this age.'

'Mm...'

Philomi sat on the doorstep of the passageway. Sebasti's two little sons were on her lap. They simply didn't have the heart to leave this beloved aunt of theirs.

'Elei... can't you sit down on the floor? Poor thing, she's still weak,' Sebasti chided them.

Cruz heaved a deep sigh and said, 'What ties do I have on this earth, now that she has gone?' He fell silent after that. In the evening, Sebasti got ready to leave with his wife and children. In spite of Sebasti's protests, Philomi changed her clothes and walked up to the bus stand with them to see them off. When they got on the bus, she too felt like going with them. There would be no ammai when she returned home. Why go home when Mariammai, who scolded her for every little thing, was no longer there? When she was about to board the bus, Sebasti's wife who hardly spoke to anyone said, 'Philomi, from now on you are your appachi's only support. You must take care of yourself too... the Lord will guide us all. We'll get going then...'

The bus left. The children kept waving their hands out of the window till the bus went some distance. Her heart ached with longing as she stood watching and she could bring herself to return home only after the bus receded into a tiny speck and disappeared from her view. On her way home, all sorts of thoughts rose and fell in her mind. She thought of Mariammai. No longer would the house ring with her commands and restrictions. One of these days, Samidas – ammai had never liked him – would attend the Sunday service with his wife. Would she be upset then? But what was there to feel upset about? Did she know only Samidas in this world? Ranji, Tharaganaar mama, next door Catherine akka, her own Amalorpavam akka, her beloved Sebasti annan – she had them all, didn't she? Besides, there was her appachi. Could it be said that her appachi had no love for her? And yet… she could never forget Samidas. That was the truth. She would live like her ammai then, like her ammai and the schoolmaster… she would always think of Samidas with the same old affection. He would remain entrenched in her heart forever, no matter how old she grew. She would always be able to understand him. Many responsibilities awaited her at home now. The big task of comforting her appachi confronted her. She would console him, assuage his grief and send him to sea. Once again, their front yard would be redolent of fish drying in the sun. More than anything, her ammai would be by her side; she would watch over everything and issue orders.

First of all, the house must be brought to some order. It overflowed with memories; not to mention the heaps of dirty clothes and dust. She must take some money from the spice box, give it to her appachi and send him to the toddy shop. Drinking would make him forget ammai. Didn't Sebasti annan take to toddy to forget Ranji when she got married? If there was no toddy shop in the seafront, the paravars would all be dead by now, fighting among themselves. True, her school teacher had taught her that drinking toddy was harmful, but what other way was left? How was it possible to rise up and get on with life without forgetting anything?

As she walked down the school street, she kept looking at the schoolmaster's house without being conscious of it. Some four or five white leghorn hens were scratching about in the front yard. The schoolmaster lived in a fairly big house. She caught a glimpse of someone reclining on a chair behind the iron railings of the veranda. It was the schoolmaster. No sooner she crossed the house, than she heard someone call out her name. Philomi turned to look. Holding on to one of the pillars of the veranda, the schoolmaster was waving his arm, beckoning her. Philomi simply stood there, hesitating for a moment. Wasn't he after all the schoolmaster who had enthralled her ammai? Philomi walked up to his house. 'Come in,' he greeted her. He always wore an eight-yard dhoti, with a bit of the upper half rolled down like a waistband. As he walked in front of her, the hens scattered away. Philomi kept standing at the doorstep. He went in, fetched a stool, and wiping it clean with his palms, asked her to sit. He then went and sat on his chair with his feet up. Feeling shy, Philomi shrank into a corner of the stool. He kept looking at her for a while. Philomi lowered her head demurely.

'I saw you going with them.'

'Yes… annan left for his village.'

They fell silent after that, as if they had nothing more to

converse about. 'Has your appachi started going to sea?' he asked after sometime.

'No, he's at home.'

'What will you eat? Let me see what I have. There are some biscuits… you must have some.' He got up and went in.

Philomi had been to that house a couple of times. When she was old enough to go to school, her ammai had brought her to the schoolmaster and it was with him that she first went to school. She had been to his house on one or two occasions after that. As for the matter between her ammai and the schoolmaster, whatever she knew of it was purely her own surmise after she grew up, what she put together from the bits and pieces of gossip that went around in the village. Appachi didn't like the schoolmaster one bit. Philomi knew that the schoolmaster had no one to call his own. He had been living by himself all these years. Except for a friend called Mariammai, he was wanted by none.

He brought the biscuits on a plastic plate and placed it on her lap. Philomi sat looking at him, her eyes full of emotions beyond words.

'Eat… what are you looking at? Appachi won't know. Come, eat… perhaps like her appachi, Philomi doesn't like me either.'

'No, no. I like you.'

He laughed loudly. Confused, Philomi raised her head and looked at him. 'You're just like your mother. She used to speak the same way too,' he said and sat staring at the doorway facing the street. His chest heaved up and down.

Philomi sat still, not wishing to disturb him. Recovering himself in a while, he said, 'Your appachi will be searching for you, won't he? If you happen to come this way, look in on this schoolmaster. When I see you, I feel as if I'm seeing your ammai. She looked just the same when she was your age. Don't know how many more years I'll be around. Only do stop by now and then.'

Philomi rose.

'I'll get going then.'

'Mm.'

Her walked with her to the street. He stood for a while, watching her go and then went in.

8

Philomi braced herself dispassionately for everything in life. Just how she was able to do that, she herself didn't understand. She kept hearing Mariammai's voice, her rebukes, every now and then – while she went about the household chores, as she dried fish in the front yard, when she stood watching the distant sea from the backdoor and while drawing water from the well. Though Mariammai was no longer alive, her memories pervaded the house.

When she set out to the seafront at dawn, Philomi felt the urge to wake her ammai up and take leave of her. At last, Cruz was able to go back to sea. The front yard reeked of fish drying in the sun, as of yore. Yet, he remained aloof and taciturn. He told his sorrow to none and withdrew into himself, suffering quietly.

After Sebasti left for his village, he wrote them a card. In it he didn't fail to reiterate that his appachi and Philomi kutty must come and live with him. Amalorpavam akka wrote her a lengthy letter. Philomi stored them all carefully in her green trunk box. She took the letters out and read them every now and then. Mariammai's trunk lay just as seashore that day, all set to embark into the sea. The sea was very choppy. The full-throated, gutsy cries of the men as they lowered the vallams into the sea and pushed them against the waves thundered past the shore and shook the adjoining coconut groves. This was nothing new. It was a familiar sight at the seafront. Launching the vallams into the sea against the might of the waves was no easy chore. All the same, they went about it as if it were a child's play. In truth, it was very, very tough.

Only the oarsmen knew the way of the waves. One look at the fold of the waves was enough to gauge its speed. There were two clever oarsmen on Rosario's launch. Rosario himself was a seasoned oarsman. Nobody had taught them. None had taught their fathers and grandfathers either. Yet, they somehow knew all they had to know about the sea. They knew, for instance, that if the surf was heavy, the mid-sea was in a churn.

Someone had scribbled lewd messages on Rosario's launch in charcoal, insinuating that his wife Victoria was carrying on with the pastor. That there was a close rapport between Rosario's family and the pastor's family was known to everyone. Rosario found it unbearable that someone had scrawled such a message, playing on the affection between the two families.

'Which son of an adulterous wretch scrawled this?' he fumed, as he cupped the seawater in his palms over and over again and sloshed it angrily over the charcoal marks in a bid to wipe them. Isaac, who stood on the shore watching this, laughed aloud. Rosario turned to look. Realizing that it been after she had opened it the last time to take out sari she had worn to church on Christmas. Philomi ope it one day. There was a bottle of cowries – big, well-roun ones – among the clothes. Not a single day had Phil seen her ammai take those cowries out or play a game dice with them. A few *thazhampoo* petals lay at the bott of the box spreading their heady fragrance. There was an notebook full of floral embroidery patterns drawn in pen Inside the notebook, she found an old, faded photogra of the schoolmaster attired in a coat, taken perhaps wh he was very young. On seeing these, a different picture her ammai emerged in Philomi's mind and she rose in h esteem.

At the seafront, little scuffles kept breaking out fro time to time between the vallams and the launche Thankfully, none of these petty fights ended in murd Still, an inexplicable pall of gloom lay on the hearts of t parakudi women. And just as they had feared, an incide occurred at the seafront one day.

There were just three fishermen on Rosario Fernandez launch – *Blue Flower* – other than him. Usually, ten or mor fishermen put to sea on the *Blue Flower*. The wages wer good. Despite that, some seven or eight men from Periy Thaazhaiyur village working on the *Blue Flower* had lef for Isaac's launch. They didn't go on their own though Isaac was a cunning man. He enticed them by offering to pay a quarter of a rupee more than what they earned on Rosario's launch. It was some three or four days after this had transpired. The launches stood majestically on the

Rosario was watching him, Isaac covered his mouth with his palm and continued to smirk and chuckle. His shoulders shook as he did so. Rosario walked straight up to Isaac, and facing him squarely asked, 'Why do you laugh, you rotten scum?'

Isaac's laughter died on hearing these words.

'Mind your words. What has happened now that you fling such words at me?'

'Did you write that?'

'Who knows?'

'Look here, I'm asking you…'

'Why ask me when there are so many fellows in this village?'

'Why did you laugh then?'

'That's none of your business. In any case, this is not your house and not your bedroom either.'

All the pent-up hatred Rosario felt towards Isaac surged in a torrent and flooded his entire being, throwing him into a fit of rage. His body trembled and his face grew red.

'When did you see my bedroom?'

'Must I see it? Isn't it enough that the whole village is talking about it?' Isaac answered him dismissively, not even looking at his face.

'Then you must have written it. You're always out to ruin people's lives. Despite knowing that you can't call over men working on other launches and vallams without the consent of the owners, you still had the gall to do that…' Rosario grabbed Isaac by his hair and twisted his head around. Isaac wondered how Rosario could muster so much strength at his age. He tried to break free from his grasp, but Rosario pushed him down on the sand and kicked him hard in his groin. Isaac collapsed but by then a few vallam owners close by came running and pulled Roasario away. Isaac staggered up, shook the sand off the back of his palms and shouted vindictively, 'Elei… see if I don't carry your wife off and outrage her in the street.' Livid with anger, Rosario struggled to break free, but the vallam owners restrained him. Not many set out to sea that day.

The seaside lay deserted one afternoon, a couple of days after this incident. The parakudi was quiet. Only the waves of the sea clamoured restlessly. Sea cormorants circled the sky over the sea, searching for food. Country boats and vallams lay criss-cross on the sands all along the shoreline. It was not yet time for them to set out to sea. The launches, which had triggered so much hostility and ill-will among the paravars, were docked in a row, bobbing up and down in the water. Rosario's launch was moored in the west end of the shore. Isaac's lay berthed in the east while Samidas' appachi's launch was in the centre. Isaac's launch was the biggest of them all. It had a cabin in the centre.

In that torpid afternoon hour, Isaac's launch suddenly caught fire and was soon aflame. In a little while, torturous wisps of smoke curled upward, as if to touch the sky.

It was church street Periya Mamiya who first noticed the fumes from the launch. Hers was the last house abutting the sea on that street. She was sitting on a palm cot at her doorstep, her legs outstretched, carefully sewing up the rents in the sari she had bought the previous Christmas.

There was no use in patching up that frayed sari. Still, she went about mending it without giving up hope. Once or twice, she even pricked her fingers with the needle, thanks to her failing eyesight. Suddenly, the needle slipped and fell from her fingers. When she bent down to search for it, her gaze fell on the seashore. It was then she saw the smoke billowing from the launch. At first, she wasn't sure if it was smoke. But very soon the acrid smell of burning timber wafted through the air. She had a very sharp nose. She shouted. Then bawling and screaming hoarsely, she ran up and down the street. Everyone stood watching her through their windows and the palm frond screens in front of their houses. They exchanged glances, wondering what had happened to Periya Mamiya. Not one of them believed what she said. As if to humour her, Carlos finally came out into the street and looked up at the sky. He saw thick, black smoke billowing from the sea.

Soon, the entire parakudi gathered at the seashore. Isaac was not at home. He was at the toddy shop with Cruz. One of Isaac's fishermen ran and gave him the news. Isaac stared hard at Rosario who sat swigging a pitcher of toddy. At that moment, the fire guzzling the launch crept up Isaac's eyes. He always carried a sharp doubled-edged knife with him. On no account did he part with it. Pulling the beautiful knife out of its leather sheath, he sprang on Rosario.

'You ill-bred scum, drinking toddy here, are you, after setting my launch on fire?' he shouted as he drove the knife hard in to the right side of Rosario's chest covered with thick greying hair. Blood spurted out. There was blood all over

Isaac. Isaac stabbed Rosario once again in the stomach and pushed him down. His body fell on the sandy floor of the toddy shop. Cruz and a few others who rushed to stop Isaac also suffered some cuts and bruises in the bargain.

That day the Manalpattur church bell tolled forty-two times. Rosario, who was dead, was just forty-two years old.

***

For nearly a week after Rosario's death, their daily life ground to a halt. Isaac turned mad. After stabbing Rosario to death, he had rushed straight to the seashore to see his burning launch. He stood staring wildly, as his dreams went up in flames.

To his frenzied mind, it seemed that Catherine was on the burning deck, clad in a blue sari, looking like an angel. A sky-blue muslin bridal veil cascaded down a small golden tiara on her head. Catherine, who had put up with his beatings and abuses all these years, had finally found her peace or so it seemed to him. She was going to her Lord. 'You mustn't die Cathri… I want you…' Isaac screamed, as he ran towards the burning launch. Surprised, everyone held him back and dragged him away. It was precisely at that moment that he had turned insane.

Philomi, who had braved far greater heartaches and misfortunes, consoled a stupefied Catherine who kept asking herself why it had all happened. The police arrested Isaac regardless of his madness and the case went to court.

Pavulu Paatta's sorrow was too deep to be assuaged by

words. Wasn't he after all their elder? An exceptional and trustworthy soul, he partook of the joys and sorrows of all the families in the parakudi as if they were his own. 'Rosario died unfortunately because of the launch. These launches – they will be the ruin of the paravars. Like the Biblical Judas, these confounded things have come to wreck our homes. Didn't our fathers and forefathers set out to sea on vallams? The fools think they can sail swiftly on these and come back laden with fish. But greed ends only in death and destruction. And it has already claimed Rosario's life. Don't know who's next...' he kept telling everyone.

9

The Christian festival of harvest and thanksgiving arrived, unmindful of what went on in the village. A red silken cloth, laced with tinsel, fluttered on the tall flagpole in front of the church. Services were held morning and evening every day.

Almost all the houses were bursting at the seams with visiting relatives. Girls, married and now settled in the neighbouring villages, came visiting with their husbands. The womenfolk of the village knew the knack of receiving one and all without so much as a murmur. The girls who had come dressed in skirts and blouses for the previous festival, now sported half-saris, looking as if by some magic spell they had grown into angels descended from the skies. For girls, this blossoming into womanhood is an enchanting experience. That moment always transpires suddenly, just like that, taking them by surprise. It could happen even as they are happily engrossed in a game of *dhaayam* or *kilianthattu* with their friends. And from then on, they come to acquire all the bashfulness and grace they have so far lacked, which is amusing indeed.

Ranji had come down for the festival as well. Only no one visited Philomi's house. Sebasti had made it his habit to visit them for the harvest festival even after his marriage but that year he had written that he would not be able to make it. In all the years after her marriage, Amalorpavam had never once visited them during the harvest festival. Philomi sat under the low thatched eaves overhanging the thinnai of her house, watching the other houses on the street overflowing with festive gaiety. It was the eighth day of the celebrations. The sapparam – the decorated chariot carrying the figurine of Mother Mary – would set forth from the church that evening and go around the streets in a procession. The expenses for the fish given as a ritual offering to the church that day was usually borne by the Sayibus, who were the regular wholesale agents of fish in that village. This custom has been in vogue for several years now. Even though the Sayibus were of a different faith, they observed this ritual with great piety. Cruz had gone out. Philomi sat recalling how happily they had all spent the eighth day celebrations last festival. In reminiscing, how fond the heart grows of the past.

***

The villagers had gathered in large flocks around the church flagpole to watch the sapparam begin its journey. The sweets and savouries push carts and makeshift bangle stalls that had mushroomed in front of the church buzzed with people. There was nothing but joy all around. Bullock carts that had arrived from the neighbouring villages lay unhitched in the ground and alleyways flanking the church. Families sat chatting in large and small knots on the jamukkalams spread under these carts.

Walking along the seashore, Philomi and Samidas left the festive crowd far behind them and sat down on the sands on the outskirts of the village. They could still hear the pleasant hum of the bustling festive crowd above the murmur of the sea. The milky glow from the tube lights fitted all around the church appeared like a haze of white smoke from that distance. The full moon was just two days away. For a long time, they lay on the sands locked in a tight embrace, as if nothing in the world could separate them. From time to time, the waves rushed under their feet as if to steal a glance at them and then beat a quick retreat, dissolving into the sea. The bullock carts which were late for the festival jingled along the dusty cart tracks, appearing and disappearing every now and then from view behind a belt of coconut palms along the shore. The place was otherwise deserted.

They lay so close, gazing at each other, that their breaths mingled. Samidas did not take advantage of their intimacy, though. But Philomi willingly took his arm and held it in a tight clasp around her shoulder. She somehow felt reassured by it. So touched was she by his self-restraint that her heart was overcome by a fierce, unconditional love for him at that very instant. She savoured the strong odour of perspiration that rose from his shirt. It sent her into raptures and made her dizzy like the heady fragrance of a million jasmines. She stroked his moustache and rubbed her face lovingly against the hair on his chest. He meant the whole world to her and the world now lay in her hands, she thought. She grew oblivious to everything else, even to the fact that she lived in a house in that village that now twinkled at a distance. After a long time, she willingly pressed her dark lips against his. His restraint, even at that moment, anguished her. She wished she could simply give herself up to Kadal Ammai and fade into the sea that very same night.

As they were walking back to the village, her head resting on his shoulder, firecrackers lit up the sky way above the towering coconut palms and came down in a shower of colourful sparks, signalling that the sapparam had at last set forth from the church street.

She would never agree to give up Samidas. She could bear anything but that. But then, why would this wish of her come true when none of her other wishes had? Philomi finally reached home. She was so overcome that she leaned against the pillar of the thinnai and wept silently. The street was now astir with people going to the church. She didn't even light the lamp. It was so comforting, sitting there in the darkness. She wished the darkness which engulfed everything would swallow her too. She heard the creak of the bamboo gate and someone walking in. It was Cruz, returning from the toddy shop.

'Alas, the sun has gone down and the vallam is struggling alone at sea,' he hummed an old song and called out her name.

'All the houses in the village are bright and lit up… but this good-for-nothing kutty can't even light a single lamp… Etee… Philomi!' Coughing, he slumped on the cot in the yard. Philomi looked at him with tears in her eyes.

'Yesuve… must I bear all the miseries by myself? Why do you heap so much suffering on me at this age, Lord!' he lamented loudly. Cruz rambled on and on, even as he coughed. 'That adulterous Maria, as long as she was alive, she kept going to that schoolmaster. Looks like this kutty has already gone in search of her man. Let these wretches carry on with whoever they please, what do I care? I have my vallam and there are fish in the sea…'

Philomi didn't feel angry, instead, she looked pitifully at him as he tossed and turned on the cot. How did their life come to this within the blink of an eye? How many things had come to pass in this last year? Philomi shuddered. Without lighting the lamp, she went inside, fetched a blanket and covered him.

Wishing to forget everything for a while, she locked the house and placed the key on the doorframe. Wrapping the end of her sari over her shoulders, she covered her head with it and stepped out into the street. Some four or five dogs were fighting at the street corner. She stood watching them, not even aware of what she was doing. She felt a strong urge to see Ranji. She was sure that Ranji would have come down for the festival. She reached Ranji's house. Only a small night lamp glowed in an alcove on the outer wall of the house. Ranji's grandmother sat munching betel leaves on a cot nearby, scarcely aware of Philomi's presence. Ranji's grandmother was a little hard of hearing. Philomi found it amusing that the entire family had gone out, trusting that decrepit old woman to watch over the house. She walked up to her, bent close to her ear and asked, 'Paatti, where are

Ranji and the others?'

'Who are you, child?'

'It's me, Philomi…'

'Who? Mariammai's youngest daughter?'

'Yes, where's Ranji?'

'Whom are you searching for? Your friend, eh? She has gone to the church with her husband. They have all gone… Only I'm here… old hag that I am, not yet dead. By the way, why are you going so late… eh?'

With great difficulty Philomi hid her feelings and said softly, 'I'll get going then, paatti.' She came out to the street and started walking. She didn't feel like going to the church anymore. It would be impossible to brush aside her memories if she went there. The streets were almost empty but for a few stragglers here and there. Philomi's heart was no longer with her; memories, a jumble of memories in no particular order took over her. She found it hard to push them away. 'Who is that? Philomi?' Startled, she broke out of her reverie. She was astonished to find herself standing in front of the schoolmaster's house.

'Come in. Why do you stand at the gate? Didn't you go to the church?'

'No…' she said as she followed him into the house without demur.

'How come you are here at this hour? Your appachi… isn't he at home?'

'Mm… he is. I just felt like taking a walk. So, I came over.'

'Are you all right? Is anything the matter?'

'No, nothing.'

'No, you look troubled. What is it? Only if you share your heart's burden will you feel better.'

They sat talking for a long time that night. She sorely wanted to confide in him, to tell him everything. She was happy she had found a new friend, someone willing to suffer and rejoice with her. The schoolmaster was making his way gently into her heart, into a corner hitherto untrodden by any feet. After a while, they ate some fruit and cake he had in his cupboard.

Philomi rose to go just about the time the sapparam returned to the church. He got up, fetched his shirt and set out with her. As he locked the house, he asked her to hold his shirt for him, a gesture that gladdened Philomi to no end. He no longer considered her a stranger, she thought. As he wore his shirt after locking the house and walked out with her, Philomi felt as if she had known him for a long, long time. Despite her protests, he accompanied her all the way to her house. As he left, she stood watching him until he turned the street corner. On entering their front yard, she saw that Cruz still lay on the cot like a corpse. She opened the front door, walked cheerfully into the house and lighted the lamp. What had been her state of mind that evening and how happy she was now. She was surprised herself. What a great miracle transpires in the heart when you let go of the past!

She knew how to whistle. When they were children, she and Ranji whistled whenever they chanced to walk together. Ranji could whistle entire songs. Though she was no match for Ranji, Philomi could whistle fairly well. She now went to the backyard whistling softly. Four or five men walked by, carrying their nets and talking among themselves. They were setting out to sea. Cruz would not be able to go fishing that day as it was already late. The day would break in a while. She must tell Ranji everything in the morning. 'Ranji! Ranji! How can I possibly wait till dawn to meet you,' Philomi thought excitedly.

She looked at the sky. A thin shard, the moon was wandering among the clouds. The sight of the moon was enough to assuage her heart, no matter how great her grief. She could see the church at a distance, glimmering beyond the coconut groves. People were still milling about in some of the makeshift stalls that had been put up just for the festival. She listened eagerly to the roar and rush of the sea. It was days since she had felt so peaceful. Henceforth, no sorrow could touch her, she thought.

She remembered to say her prayers before she lay down to sleep. Her ammai's face flashed across her mind for a second. Were she still alive, would her ammai approve of her visit to the schoolmaster? Ammai would have been very happy about it, no doubt at all.

Mariammai often remarked that if you fell asleep listening to the murmur of the sea, you woke up feeling light and chirpy. The sea was truly extraordinary, like Ranji, like the Tharaganaar, like the schoolmaster. It sent out its benediction to everyone through its sprightly waves; their clamour was nothing but a proclamation of joy. Philomi fell asleep listening to the loud crash of the surf.

10

As it happened, Ranji herself came to Philomi's house the next day. The two friends went to their usual haunt – the well in the backyard – and sat chatting. First, Ranji asked Philomi about her ammai's death. Ranji didn't care much for such formalities. Nevertheless, she condoled with Philomi on her misfortune. Ranji was with child and her belly was noticeably big now. So many things had come to pass over those two months. Philomi stroked her belly lovingly. A strange, shimmering beauty now hung about Ranji, though she looked a little weak. Perhaps, it was this languorous exhaustion which gave her that delicate glow. Philomi looked at her with yearning, as though she couldn't get enough of her. How did this Ranji come to look so beautiful all of a sudden? It was all simply beyond her.

'Ranji, know how lovely you look?'

Overcome by a touch of coyness, Ranji lowered her head and looked bashfully at Philomi. Philomi gave her an ardent hug and kissed her. 'Why Ranji, I wouldn't let go of you were you a man,' she teased. They then fell talking and Philomi couldn't stop telling her about the schoolmaster.

Need Philomi speak at length? Wasn't Ranji, after all, a perceptive woman? She didn't look surprised at all and listened casually as if to say, 'well, so it is!' Somehow, she was deeply familiar with the strange propensities of the heart. Those good old days she had passed in Sebasti's company – it was then that she had grown wise to the delicate pathways of the heart undefiled by any feet. Ranji concluded that Philomi nurtured a deep affection for the schoolmaster. A smile played on her lips, 'You sly thing! How quickly your heart succumbs to friendship and affection,' she mused.

'What Ranji, why do you smile?' Philomi asked her.

'Nothing…'

'Come, you stubborn thing, I know you wouldn't smile without reason.'

'So, you have grown very fond of the schoolmaster then?' Ranji asked her, smiling.

'Yes, he's a nice man… only appachi can't stand the sight of him.'

'Good then. One way or another, you should be happy… only that will put my heart at ease.'

Philomi took Ranji into the kitchen and placed a reed mat on the floor. Seizing Ranji's hands, she bade her sit and Ranji obeyed just like a child. Reminiscing about the old days, Philomi made some black coffee, hot enough for Ranji's liking. Thoroughly drenched in Philomi's love, Ranji drank it in wordless silence. When it was time for her to leave, she manged to get up with great difficulty, holding on to Philomi's outstretched hand. When she held on to Philomi's hand, Ranji felt her heart choke. That hand – how it lavished love on everyone. Can you put a price on such love and affection? Even if she were to give the sea that clamoured outside the house in return, would it be a just recompense? This fondness for someone, this friendship – how do such feelings blossom of their own accord? The cruellest among men – haven't they ever experienced such friendship, haven't they ever come across such a loving hand? Friendship and love – these matters of the heart are vast and profound, like the sea. It is with things such as these that our tenuous hold on life lies magically intertwined. No matter how terrible life is, no matter how dreadful its course, no one here wishes to die, thanks to such friendships and affections.

Philomi locked her house and accompanied Ranji to her house. Ranji introduced Philomi to her mother-in-law and father-in-law.

On several nights, Ranji had spoken about Philomi to her husband. Needless to say, the minute he saw her, he surmised that she was Ranji's Philomi. He had only seen her at a distance once or twice and had never really met her. He stared at her in amazement, wondering what Ranji had found in her that she kept prattling endlessly about her. As a matter of fact, Philomi was darker in complexion than Ranji. What he found alluring about her though were her dark lips. He couldn't take his eyes off them. Even Samidas was smitten by her lips. For all that, Philomi's lips were very small. But her lower lip had a certain lustre about it. Perhaps it was this that these men were attracted to. What did the schoolmaster like about Philomi? Was it just her dark lips? Was it their allure that had made him accompany her all the way to her home the other night? Perhaps. All said and done, who could say that Philomi's lips weren't beautiful?

Ranji's husband enquired after everyone in Philomi's house. He had a remarkable voice. It was as sweet as the organ music played by the choirmaster when they all emerged from the church after the service. But his physique, how rugged and rough-hewn it was. And that big, burly figure was all Ranji's to keep. That figure and that voice, how utterly discordant they were. That day too Philomi went home feeling very happy. But then, do all days turn out to be so pleasant?

***

How did the sea know the arrival of the new moon day? It rolled and pleated its huge waves and rushed forward to unfurl them in display to the vast sandy shores and then drew them back safely into its depths. Even the wind seemed to have somehow got a whiff of all this. The sea and the darkness- how they danced together. The sea was in a churn, seething with tumultuous excitement.

Just when Periya Mamiya was about to sit down to have her meal, the wind smothered the only lamp she had lighted that evening in a loving embrace. Cursing the wind, she groped for the box of matches under the bamboo poles of the rafters. As she struck a match and lighted the lamp again, she heard someone singing in the darkness of the coconut grove behind her house. Her eyes, creased and wrinkled with age, widened in surprise. She placed her ear close to thatched wall of her hut and listened. She could still hear the song. Pushing the door of her hut open, she came out holding the lamp and looked around. She drew the wick of the lamp out as the flame fluttered in the wind, and went around to back of the hut. Startled by the light, a stray *Kombai* dog lying there, tilted its head, looked at Mamiya and with a look of boredom, buried its face once again between its legs. In the light of the lamp, the shadow of the coconut trees fell on the sand in long, undulating lines. When Periya Mamiya walked, her hands and head quivered and faint sounds, like the whimpering of a kombai dog, rose from her. She walked in the direction of the song. A tall and hefty man lay stretched out on the sand, singing. It was an old ditty sung by the paravars. He kept singing unawares, till Periya Mamiya went close to him. She held the lamp over his face and peered down to have a better look. Periya Mamiya recognized him and cried out in surprise, 'You son of a sinner, you're Isaac, aren't you?'

Isaac fixed his gaze on Mamiya, stared hard at her, and smiled slowly as if he recognized her. 'Elei, why do you lie here in the dead of night, son? Shouldn't you go home?' Periya Mamiya asked him. Isaac simply continued singing from where he had left off. Mamiya stood next to him for a little while, then turned and hobbled away. 'How this fellow lived and what has he come to now!' she shook her head and muttered, as she walked.

The case filed against Isaac by the Kulasekara Pattinam police was acquitted on the grounds that the murder had been committed in a drunken fit. As for Catherine, her maternal uncle came down and took her away. Isaac, however, stayed back, haunting day and night the stretch of shore where his launch had once stood. He often stood staring vacantly at the sea. Now there were only three launches on the Manalpattur seashore.

As usual, the launches set out to sea with the vallams and other country boats. The launches swept past the vallams to distant places where there was plenty of fish and consequently, a fierce and ugly rivalry raged between them at sea. There were several nasty skirmishes and the only thing that didn't happen as yet was a paravan being murdered mid-sea. Only Pavulu Paatta was anxious and worried for everyone.

A village committee meeting was called for one day to discuss the matter but no one was willing to make any compromise. As days passed, the vallams made smaller and smaller hauls. Soon, they were not even able to give the fish due to the agents in lieu of the interest they owed them.

The three launches, however, always returned laden with catch. Rosario's son Lazar turned out to be much cleverer than his father. He brought over new fishermen for their launch, the *Blue Flower*, from Kulachal. Even Siluvai kept harping that he might leave for Samidas' appachi's launch. There was no way Cruz could pay him more. If truth be told, Philomi was the only reason why Siluvai hadn't left. He was simply waiting for the right time. When the moment came, he planned to make off with Philomi. So what if he was married? True, he already had two children through Innasi. But then, how did it matter? He simply couldn't wipe out from his heart the picture of Philomi sleeping face down every time he went to Cruz's house to fetch the fishing nets in the evening.

As it happened, one day when Cruz was not at home Siluvai went over to fetch the nets. Philomi, who had stretched down to sleep at noon, still lay in deep slumber. He stood at the doorstep looking at her. Her sari had slipped off her shoulder and her legs were bare up to her knees; her dusky, sinuous figure and youthfulness enticed him. Though she was fast asleep, it was strange that her womanly instincts should be awake. She woke up with a start. On seeing Siluvai standing there, his eyes inflamed with passion, she got up hastily and flung her sari over her shoulder. He smiled sheepishly.

'What do you want?'

'Hee hee… isn't appachi at home?'

'Can't you see he's not here? Isn't that why you've been standing here so long, staring at a sleeping woman?'

'No, I came just now.'

'Who knows?'

'If appachi comes, tell him Siluvai has already left with the net,' he said, as he walked away. Philomi didn't feel angry at him; instead, she pitied him.

Finally, a bride from Idinthakarai was chosen for Samidas and the marriage fixed. These days Philomi went to church on Sundays with Ranji. Ranji's husband had returned to Uvariyur after leaving her at her parent's house for her confinement.

One Sunday, Samidas' entire family came to the church.

Samidas wore a new dhoti. His appachi and ammai went into the church ahead of him while his thatha sat down on the corridor. Only Samidas stood outside talking to his friends. Philomi and Ranji entered the church compound just then. It was Ranji who spotted Samidas first and she drew Philomi's attention to him. For a minute, Philomi stood rooted to the spot. Samidas noticed her too but wanting to avoid her eyes, he turned away and stood with his back to her. Philomi thought that he looked very handsome that day. On seeing his sister Dorothy walking from the direction of the church well, Philomi called out to her, 'Sh sh… Dorothy, come here.' She too wore a new blouse and half-sari. 'Ei, your annan hardly ever comes to church, why is he here today?' Philomi asked her anxiously. Deep inside her heart, she had fathomed it all and yet, she asked. Ranji kept looking at Samidas who was still talking to his friends.

'Don't you know then, akka? Annan is going to have his wedding banns called today. Come in, why are you both standing out? Do you want to talk to annan?'

'No… what is there to talk to him about now?'

Philomi dissolved into tears.

'Ranji, must we go in? I simply can't bear to go in. I'm going home,' Philomi lowered her head and turned to leave. Ranji caught hold of her hand. Samidas was watching everything. Only his heart cried out, 'Philomi… my dearest Philomi.'

'Leave me Ranji, let me go.'

Ranji smiled sadly. Only Ranji could smile in the midst of any sorrow.

'No, you must come in. You must hear the banns being called for your Samidas' wedding. After all, who can be dearer to him? Mustn't you know who his bride is? Just come in.' She tugged Philomi along by her arm. Wiping her eyes with the end of her sari, Philomi followed her.

Deeply touched, Samidas stood looking at Philomi as she entered the church. His sister Dorothy did not fully comprehend the situation. Perplexed, she kept turning her head around to look at Philomi and Ranji.

Ranji had put Philomi in a very distressing situation. She was choking with tears. She couldn't even weep aloud, to her heart's content. The pastor read out some verses from the Bible and said, 'The first reading from the Gospel of the Lord is over.' Fortunately, Philomi and Ranji were seated in the last row. In a way, it was very convenient. Ranji chided Philomi in hushed tones every now and then, 'Sh sh… What's this? Look at you, weeping like a child. Now that everything is over, can't you let it be? Didn't you see him standing there like a stone? Did he even say a word to you? And here you are, crying your heart out like a child for him…' She wiped Philomi's tears discreetly.

The congregation stood up and sang, 'Why this agony my Lord, what can I give you in return…' It seemed to Philomi that everyone was singing for her. Her ammai used to sing that song very often. Ranji sang with all her heart, as if she was intent on dissolving all her sorrows in the song. Her voice quivered and choked. The impenetrable anguish that filled it was beyond words.

The pastor began reading out the wedding banns after

the song. As music from the organ played by the choirmaster wafted all over the church, the pastor read,

> Chellakkanni Clarinda, the daughter ofTimothy and the granddaughter of Isaiah Fernandez belonging to the parish of Idinthakarai and Samidas, Lazar Fernandez's second son and Gabriel Fernandez's grandson belonging to the parish of Manalpattur are to be joined in Holy Matrimony on the 16th of March. If any of you know any cause or just impediment, why these two persons should not be joined together in holy matrimony, you are to declare it.

Ranji glanced at Philomi. Philomi was looking out through the window, her gaze rivetted on Samidas' face. He too stood with tears in his eyes. He was seized by an impulse to run up to Philomi, to pull her by her hand and march up to the pastor and declare, 'I'm deeply in love with this girl. I'll marry only her.' Had at least Philomi stood up and objected, the wedding would have been called off. But she didn't.

Once the service was over, Ranji and Philomi walked out as if nothing had happened. When they turned the corner of the church street, Philomi said, 'Ranji I want to take the path by the seashore today, come with me.' Yielding to her wish, Ranji walked with her through the coconut groves towards the seashore. The Tharaganaar stood in his grove. Coconut picking was on in full swing in his grove that day and he was overseeing his men.

They were silent as they walked along the seashore. Philomi recounted her reminiscences to those waves. One after the other, the waves tumbled ashore, listened to what she said and drew back. When they reached her house, she turned to Ranji and said, 'Ranji, it's all over now, isn't it? What's there to worry about, henceforth?'

11

A week later, Cruz came home one day in a fluster. Philomi was sitting on the thinnai reading her hymn book after many, many days.

'Kutty, my child…' he called out as he came in. That was how he addressed her whenever he was happy.

'I must talk to you about something,' he said as he sat down on the thinnai next to her. He lovingly straightened a few strands of loose hair that fell on her face. He gently stroked her back. He seemed to have at last remembered these demonstrations of affection. After so many days it had occurred to him that he must shower his love and care on her. He was not drunk that day. Philomi was baffled.

'What is it, appachi?'

Cruz kept staring at his dark, calloused palms for a while. Philomi noticed that constant rowing had left the skin on his palms stiff, like thick cardboard.

'We can't eke out a living here any longer. There's no way we can catch fish on this old vallam of ours as in the past. It doesn't suit us vallam owners to fight these launch fellows either. What can we do? Ever since your ammai died, this house has been slowly crumbling apart. Not that you don't know any of this. This sea will no longer feed the poor and the wretched. It stands terrified by man's stubbornness. Some six to seven families from the middle street and the church street have already packed their bags and moved out. What's left of your uncle's house is a pitiful rubble. They say his mother-in-law lay dead inside the palm thickets without a drop of gruel to appease her hunger. Tch… but why am I telling you all these cursed tales? I've decided to sell the vallam. Our Siluvai – he has offered to buy it. When I first took him out to sea, the fellow was just sixteen. Your thatha was alive then. His mother Annamaria brought him over and entrusted him to my appachi saying, 'Brother, only you must prevail upon this unlucky, fatherless fellow and bring him to some good.' And he has remained faithful to this day. He has offered me three hundred and fifty rupees for the vallam. He will hand over the money the day after tomorrow. All we need to do is pack our things from here and go away to Sebasti. As for the house, Rosario's son wants to buy it. After his appachi's death, the family has come to see good times. He'll give us a thousand one hundred as agreed within a week. Once the sale is through at the Tiruchendur Sub Registrar's office, we can get going. We should've gone as soon as your ammai died. What's left for us in this village now? This is such an ancient house. It's a pity. The vallam and this house are the only assets to stay with the family for so many generations. Now it is destined that they must come to wrack and ruin in my hands and pass out of the family. What can anyone do?' His voice trembled and broke as he said these words and the anguish of his heart rose in a flood.

'Why are you silent?'

'Appachi, your wish is my wish too,' said Philomi.

'No matter how things go, this Cruz has at least brought up his daughter to obey her appachi's words. By the way, what did you cook today… serve whatever you have,' he said. Philomi closed her book with a deep sigh and went in.

There had never been a time when Cruz had sat down inside the house to have his meal. He rarely stepped into the house. He had entered the house recently when Mariammai had died and thereafter had kept to his cot in the front yard, never setting foot inside even once. The few clothes he had, were on a clothesline in the thinnai. He usually ate his meals on the thinnai and stretched out on the string cot in the yard until it was time to set out for the catch. Before Mariammai's death, he had gone into the house on just two occasions – when Dasaiyya had passed away and prior to that, to look at Mariammai and Philomi when Philomi was born. You could easily count the number of days he had been inside the house. That day, however, he followed Philomi into the kitchen and sat down there to drink his gruel. Philomi looked at him in astonishment. That such a tender heart should lie inside him came as a surprise to her.

***

Cruz told Phiomi that she needn't write to Sebasti about the sale of the vallam and the house, presently. And he stopped going to sea. What ties did he have with the sea now? All the same, he couldn't bear not to look at it. Siluvai hadn't paid the money for the vallam as yet. But since they had already come to an agreement, Cruz permitted him wholeheartedly to take it out to sea. In the evenings, he helped Siluvai launch the vallam into the sea. He stood there for a while, watching it romp over the waves like a seahorse and only then returned home. He also arranged for Siluvai's wife's brother to help pull the oars and cast the net.

Not forgetting his old loyalty, Siluvai dropped in at Cruz's house every day to leave a portion of the catch that was left after the wholesale agents had taken their due.

Only the Tharaganaar was disconsolate that Cruz had sold his vallam. He was not in the village at that time. If only he had been around, he wouldn't have allowed it. 'The fellow has lost his mind,' he despaired over and over again. What's more, he even fought with Philomi over this. 'If you weren't able to do anything, what prevented you from coming and telling me, eh? I would've laid a slap or two on his ears at once and put an end to it, my child,' he told her.

But what did it all matter now? It was all over – the house and the vallam had been sold. When the sale deed of the house was written out in favour of Rosario Fernandez's son at the Tiruchendur Registrar office and when Cruz finally scribbled his long-forgotten signature on the document, his fingers shook. And that was the end of it all. He bought a packet of Philomi's favourite *uruttu sev* at a sweets and savouries shop in Tiruchendur, then a piece of slightly expensive blouse cloth and a nice sari for her. He didn't get anything for himself, not even a plain seam lungi. 'Where's the need for new clothes and fineries for myself now,' he told himself. When he was buying the sari, he was reminded of his Mariammai. It was remarkable how his eyes misted over with tears even at that age.

He alighted from the bus at the Manalpattur village stopping, carrying a large sum of money and yet, his heart knew no peace. He trembled all over, as if he had committed murder. He was tormented by guilt and remorse. The first person he saw, as soon as he got down from the bus, was Pavulu Paatta. He was walking westward. Holding his palm against his forehead to ward off the sun, he peered hard to see who was alighting from the bus.

'Who's that now? Cruz?' Where are you returning from?' he asked as he approached Cruz.

'I'd been to Tiruchendur.'

Pavulu Paatta shook with laughter.

'Elei, in all my years I've hardly seen you step out of this village, son. Why, what's the matter?'

For a second Cruz looked at him hesitantly and then said, 'Went to the Registrar's office there.'

'Did you clinch some nice deal or what? Perhaps, your son gave you some money?'

'No, I did the selling.'

'Elei, what are you saying? What did you sell? To whom?'

'The house, what else. To Rosario's son…'

'Mm… bits and pieces of this news reached my ears too, the other day. What… what's come over you, eh? Have you gone out of your mind or what? Have you turned insane like that Isaac next door? Crazy fellow, who'd sell such a fine house?'

Cruz wanted to desist from saying anything, but he couldn't. 'Is there anything that Paatta doesn't know? A paravan who's badly off can no longer hope to live here.'

'But must you sell the house you are living in for that?'

'What else do you ask me to do?'

'Get lost, le! Just get lost! You fellows have no faith in the sea nor the work you do. Only if you remain faithful to the sea, will it keep you well. Sooner or later, this is going to be the undoing of your lot. No wonder you have all gone off your heads… what else can I say?'

Paatta walked away, not wishing to stand there any longer. Shortly, Cruz began walking towards the village.

He grew troubled and restless. Had he really committed a grave mistake then? His heart grew ill at ease. The sun was beating down from the west. The money he had secured in the folds of his lungi weighed intolerably heavy, like a boulder. The paper parcel under his arm containing the uruttu sev and the new sari he had bought for Philomi turned soggy with his sweat.

As he walked, lost in thought, the frothy and spumy surf rolled and crashed on the sands before him. Without being aware of it, he had walked to the seashore, simply from force of habit. He secured his lungi firmly around his waist and tied his waist string over it like a belt. He placed the sari, uruttu sev and money in his shoulder towel and wrapped them into a bundle. His vallam lay moored in its usual spot, half-sunk in the sand, looking forlorn. Though the vallam was now in Siluvai's hands, he had pulled it ashore at the spot where Cruz usually docked it. Even if he were to haul it ashore at some other place, the vallam somehow returned to its usual haunt. It was not a live, breathing thing, true, but it was very ancient. It had always come ashore to rest in the same spot since Cruz's appachi's time. That spot was its home. It would never leave its home. And it wouldn't wish to either. Whereas man is not like that. He doesn't have faith in anything. The vallam is a living witness. It never speaks. Were you to listen to its tales, this entire parakudi will simply go up in flames. The vallams are alive to everything happening around them but remain mute spectators, considering the well-being of their owners. Even brand new launches grow rusty in the sea breeze but this plank of wood never gets rusty. It is faithful to the sea. The waves of the sea never seize the vallams and drown them in their depths. If at all they capsize in the whirlpool near Siluvaiparai, they simply drift ashore. A sea *Mohini* dwells in that whirlpool and she loves human blood or so the paravars believe. But it also happens that these paravars forget to dread her presence from time to time. Man has never triumphed in his struggle against the sea. Not realizing this, the launches set sail with noisy furore, challenging the vallams.

Cruz went nearer the vallam and caressed it longingly, as if it were a beloved child he had been parted from for ages. After all, it had partaken of all his joys and sorrows at sea, like his Mariammai, hadn't it? He was torn by grief. His chest heaved. He flung the bundle he carried on the sands beside the vallam and dropped down, his gaze resting on the sea.

Some distance away, Isaac was running, hollering at the top of his voice at something. Some four or five little boys from the parakudi ran naked behind him. As Isaac ran eastward, the waves rolled up to his feet, sniggered mockingly at him and retreated into the sea. The sea spares no one.

Though Cruz was lying on the sandy seashore, he was frightened as though he was at mid-sea, under water. It seemed to him that the waves massed and rolled over him, fold after fold. He heard the footsteps of the sea Mohini. And then, the sea swallowed him. He plummeted faster and faster towards the seabed and there was a loud rush of noise all around him. If only he didn't hear this deafening roar, he could swim up to the surface. But who could stop it? Pavulu Paatta's words rang in his ears, 'Elei, this is going to be your undoing…'

Summoning all his strength, he stood up with great difficulty, picked up his bundle and set off homeward. With each faltering step, he felt as if his legs were sinking knee-deep into the sands. 'Yesuve! Why am I heading towards the sea! My house is not here...' But try as he might, his legs strayed towards the sea. He simply couldn't turn and walk away from it. Once again, he dropped down on the sand with a loud thud. After carousing with the shores, the waves withdrew into the sea and returned over and over again to plead at Cruz's feet like his pure and innocent Philomi. They called out to him. His carefully wrapped bundle of things was thoroughly soaked by now. The beautiful sari he had bought for Philomi, her favourite uruttu sev – the sea had licked and savoured everything.

Nothing could ever happen on that seashore without Periya Mamiya being aware of it. Her back was bent with age. Her teeth had all fallen. She had portioned out her youth to the paravar fellows living on that seashore. Shrivelled with age, there was nothing left in her body. All her spirit and vital force had come to dwell in her eyes. How they glowed like live coals. From time to time, she came out of the house and placing her palm over her forehead, surveyed the seashore keenly as if someone might decamp with it any moment. Then nodding her head to herself as if to say, 'it's all right, it's all right, nothing has been stolen' she tottered back into to the house and settled down to sew her clothes. Patching up old clothes was her main chore. She went about all the time with a needle and thread in hand, as if all the clothes in her house were frayed and torn; as if she had to keep sewing them up endlessly. Mamiya knew each and every paravan living on that seashore inside out. But she never tittle-tattled about anyone. On festival days, she always managed, no matter how hard, to get drunk. Even in that frail old age she had the pluck to swig toddy and loll about in drunken stupor.

She foraged the seashore for cast-off fish. As she spread them out to be sun-dried on the sands in the coconut grove behind her house, she often broke into loud hosannas. Her frail voice quavered in the air, carrying the unbearable weight of her longings and sorrows. At such times, her neighbours remarked, 'Looks like Mamiya is in one of her moods.' She was a free spirit and so far, no one had been able to tamper with her freedom.

It was Periya Mamiya who first noticed Cruz lying on the seashore. Her sharp eyes grew wide in surprise. She hastily climbed down the sandy ridge and shaking her head, plodded across the sands. There had been a time when she could easily sprint across that sandy stretch.

Gripping Cruz by his armpits, she hoisted him up and dragged him slowly across the sands and left him near his vallam. She then fetched his bundle that lay some distance away. She placed the back of her palm under his nostrils, feeling for his breath and all at once, her mouth parted in a toothless smile. She then hurried to fetch Philomi.

Poor Cruz, he didn't die. If only he had died, his sorrows would have also perished with him.

Philomi wrote to Sebasti and her akka through the schoolmaster. It is true that certain moments in life strengthen our ties with one another. When she went up to the schoolmaster's house that day to get the letters written, she spoke without any reserve to him, as she had done once before. It was nothing grave or important. Just this and that – about small, ordinary happenings from the past. But when you looked back on them, how they shimmered with an ineffable beauty.

In the kingdom of Cruz's heart, one pathway was sealed off forever and another opened. He remembered nothing of the past. He simply did what he was told like a child. He even forgot his dear Philomi kutty. Sebasti came, though not at once. He arrived only after four or five days. Philomi didn't touch the money Cruz had with him. She handed it to the schoolmaster, asking him to keep it safe for her. The

Tharaganaar who was away at Thoothukudi on dried fish business, rushed to see Cruz after hearing the news on his return.

'I told him, didn't I. But he just wouldn't listen… If you were so badly in need of money, wouldn't I have done something about it? How can this fellow bear to part with his vallam, daughter? He has been reduced to this, at last, the poor wretch!' he despaired. 'Daughter, you mustn't hesitate to come to me if you ever need something. As long as this *Musalmaan* is alive, he won't let you shed a tear,' he consoled Philomi.

The schoolmaster dropped in every day now. It was he who assisted Philomi in everything. Sebasti came down every now and then. He felt a great responsibility towards the family now – so great that it couldn't be uttered in words. Meanwhile, Rosario's son laid claim to the house at an inopportune moment, setting fire to their already bruised hearts. But when Sebasti declared stoutly, 'This is our ancestral property. It was wrong on your part to have misled my appachi and bought it without my knowledge. I'll file a case against you,' Rosario's son backed off, frightened. Later, everyone got together and arbitrated between them. The sale was somehow annulled and the money handed back to Rosario's son. While leaving, Sebasti promised to send twenty rupees every month. Philomi merely smiled on hearing that. Amalorpavam akka had also written something to that effect. But come what may, Philomi was prepared to fight it all out.

Only Siluvai deceived them, letting down all the trust

Cruz had placed in him. When it became obvious that Cruz would no longer confront him, he declared that he had already paid up the entire sum for the vallam. Livid with rage, the Tharaganaar went up to Siluvai's house one day and thrashed him. Summoning the entire street, he lashed out at Siluvai in the most obscene language he had ever used in his lifetime.

Soon, the village was abuzz with the news of the schoolmaster's frequent visit to Philomi's house. This bit of gossip fell on Samidas' ears too. Though he was all set to marry another girl, he couldn't help feeling sad in his heart of hearts. Ranji was aware of everything, so she didn't say anything. But the Tharaganaar asked Philomi about it straight to her face one day.

'What's this mama, what have you found out that you talk like this? Must you speak like the rest of the village too?' asked Philomi.

'Tch… what do I care about this village, daughter? It's you I care about. So I shall only listen to you.'

One day Philomi told the schoolmaster, 'But for you this Philomi would have jumped into the sea and died.'

The schoolmaster laughed.

'You're saying this, but there's a talk going around the village. Are you aware of it?'

'Oh, I know, I know.'

'What do you think of that?'

Now it was Philomi who laughed.

'Having defied this village all these years, must you give ear to their idle talk now?'

'No, I've never paid heed to their talk. Even Mariammai never did. Which of these parava fellows is upright? If we pick and choose, not a single fellow will hold out. Forget that. I asked what *you* thought of all this talk.'

'You know what, I'm Mariammai's daughter.'

'Oh, is that so then? I forgot you are Mariammai's daughter. Somehow, my heart has come to believe that you are Mariammai herself,' he said laughing.

They laughed heartily. Cruz, who lay on the cot, stared as if startled by some noise and then turned away. The minute she saw Cruz, Philomi's laughter died away, as if the relentless waves of the sea had suddenly come to rest.

'Why have you fallen silent all of a sudden?'

'Nothing... appachi was looking. He doesn't remember you at all, that's why he's so docile. Earlier, once when ammai had taken ill, you had come to see her and what a hue and cry he made that day... I remembered that just now.'

'Philomi, know something? I've never felt anger towards your appachi.'

Philomi grew quiet after that. Everything seemed like a dream to her. Innumerable sorrows came looking for her. And yet, she never thought of giving up her life. She still felt very much attached to everything. True, there were times when she felt utterly lonely. She had never been able to understand herself. For that matter, when do we ever understand anyone completely? Ranji was able to relate to everyone and everything around her. She too had been let down by Philomi's brother, Sebasti. But Ranji prevailed over everything. Nothing affected her, be it triumphs or defeats.

She too lived with the burden of all her memories. But it was also the same Ranji who stepped away from everything and watched quietly from a distance. Only Ranji could be like that. Only she could have such a heart. Did Samidas deceive Philomi? All said and done, Philomi could never come to that conclusion. Something akin to hope still lived in her heart. She still nurtured the thought that Samidas would come one day and carry her away like King Prithiviraj Chauhan she had read about in her childhood. Such naïve hopes! Just the same, it was true that such hopes still dwelt in Philomi's heart. She bore no resentment towards Samidas, just as the schoolmaster harboured no anger towards Cruz.

Who was this schoolmaster? Was he her ammai's friend? What did Philomi find in him that she sought him despite all the loose talk in the village? She didn't know. She couldn't say why. For that matter, what had she found in Samidas that she loved him in spite of everything that had happened? Or come to think of it, what did she find in Ranji and the Tharaganaar?

She lay awake for a long time that night, counting the light beams that flashed and faded from the lighthouse and eventually fell asleep.

12

No matter what transpires in their waking hours, regardless of how big an occurrence, men are able to sleep at night as if nothing has happened. As for the sea, it never sleeps. Who knows if it wishes to sleep? Perhaps, the sea Mohini is wise to the sea's longings; or perhaps, the fish that swim in it. A man born in the parakudi rarely sleeps at night. When sleep pervades everything, he sets out to battle the waves and the wind. His day begins in the darkness of dawn. The paravars are the sons of the sea. And Kadal Ammai, large-hearted and merciful as she is, is as dear to them as the smiling figurine of Virgin Mary in their church.

Elderly men like Pavulu Paatta meted out justice to them like their everlasting Lord in heaven. You will find the likes of Pavulu Paatta – exceptional men born accidentally in their midst – in Ranji's husband's village or in Idinthakarai, the village where Samidas' bride came from or for that matter in all other fishing hamlets as well. It was their pure and guileless hearts that stood guard over these parakudis.

One day Pavulu Paatta came to Cruz's house, got down on his knees and said a long, heart-rending prayer. The consoling words of that elderly man gave Philomi untold strength.

Month after month, Sebasti and Amalorpavam akka sent her money as promised. Sebasti's wife didn't approve, though. But he remained firm and unyielding in this matter so much so his wife was quite surprised by it. Every time Amarlorpavam sent money, she wrote a long letter exhorting Philomi to be happy. 'Philomi, there's nothing in the hands of men. Think of the Lord, pray to Him. Nothing is impossible if the Lord wills it,' she wrote unfalteringly in letter after letter. These days, Philomi went to the church every day for the evening service. Sebasti had entreated her and his appachi to come and stay with him but Philomi refused. That the schoolmaster accompanied her to the church occasionally was indeed a matter of great surprise, for he never went to church, not even on festival days. She had brought about a change even in the schoolmaster. Life is indeed very strange. How it binds together people who hardly know each other. Philomi never prayed for herself. That Cruz should recover was her only prayer. It was just this that she implored the Lord for.

Siluvai's vallam didn't throw a tantrum, refusing to go to sea because he had deceived Cruz. After all, what does a vallam know? Or perhaps it does. Who can say?

Samidas fretted that he had deceived Philomi. He knew that all he needed to do was simply walk up to her doorstep and call out her name. Philomi would willingly follow him. But he was terrified of his appachi. If only he could avoid confronting his appachi's round, marble-like eyes, he would have gone and stood at Philomi's doorstep and called her. He couldn't forget the evening he had made love to Philomi. He had touched her several times before that. There had been times when he had even crushed her in a tight embrace, leaving her gasping for breath. And he had kissed her dark lips often. He had never considered these as inappropriate. Back then, he needed her desperately and it was as simple as that. As for Philomi, she didn't spurn him either. Little wonder that she ruled his heart. These are things to be happy about, no doubt, but money buys love in the end. If only Philomi had been a launch owner's daughter, Samidas could have happily married her.

***

Meanwhile, Ranji's husband came running to Philomi's house early one night to fetch her. Philomi and the schoolmaster were engrossed in talk when he arrived. Cruz, who lay on his cot, blinked at everyone in perplexity. Those eyes – how powerful they had once been. Sadly, only a childlike bewilderment filled them now.

'Appachi, seems Ranji is in labour. I'm just going over to her house. You look after the house.'

He nodded his head vigorously.

'Where, where? Ranji… Ranji… your Ranji's house… Ranji's house,' he kept repeating to himself, as if he was trying to recall everything that had been wiped clean from his heart.

Philomi would be of no use to Ranji at this hour and yet,

it was her that Ranji had sent for in the midst of unbearable birth throes. She somehow drew strength from the thought that she could endure worser pain if only Philomi was beside her. The schoolmaster went too. Wrapping the end of her sari tightly around her shoulders, Philomi hurried ahead of the two men. The schoolmaster and Ranji's husband chatted as they walked, like long-lost friends.

Two narrow cots lay in front of Ranji's house. A hurricane lamp hung from the wooden rafters of the thinnai. Ranji's thatha lay on one of the cots. The house swarmed with women who had come to assist in the childbirth. Ranji's *kozhundan* – her younger brother-in-law – was busy digging a furrow outside, in the ground beneath the drain hole of the birthing room. Ranji's ammai spotted Philomi as soon as she arrived.

'Give way… move aside all of you; there, her friend has come. Come, child, she has been asking for you,' she said. On hearing this, Philomi's eyes grew moist with tears. She sat gently beside Ranji and held her hands.

'Ranji… did you send for me even at this hour? Am I going to look after you more than your own people or what? Is the pain unbearable? Come, come, don't cry. Look, I'm here, by your side,' Philomi comforted her.

The village midwife shouted orders to the womenfolk. Can she go around ordering the villagers at other times? Whenever she came to assist in childbirth, her authority held sway over the entire household. In fact, she derived a peculiar satisfaction from ordering the village folk around at such times. Meanwhile, one of the women suggested that a bottle of arrack be brought to help ease the pain.

Ranji's husband, the schoolmaster, Ranji's appachi, her thatha and their neighbour Joshua sat on the cot outside the house and passed the time chatting. Ranji's kozhundan was upset that so many women had surrounded his *Madini*, making it impossible for him to have a glimpse of her. He was desperate to see her at this hour. Under the pretext of digging the furrow, he peeped into the room through the window. He managed to see Ranji's face. Even in the midst of her pain, Ranji managed to smile at him. On seeing his face, one of the women in the room shouted, 'Chee! What a shameless fellow! Is he so fond of his brother's wife? Look at him peeping in. Kozhunda pilley, why don't you drink all the dirty water that flows into the furrow!' She then slammed the window shut. This was followed by loud giggles. Just as the woman slammed the window, he caught sight of Philomi covering her mouth with the end of her sari and laughing like the rest. He felt thoroughly abashed. He just went and sat on the cot, next to the schoolmaster. It was Ranji's deep affection for him that had driven him to peep through the window so childishly but who would understand all that.

Ever since Ranji stepped into their house, he shirked going to sea and stayed put at home most of the time under the pretext of being ill. On some days, his elder brother – Ranji's husband – bathed in hot water. At such times, he found immense pleasure in lifting the huge hot water *tavalai* along with his madini. He wished he could sit chatting with her all day long. And Ranji indulged him. As for Ranji's husband, whatever was her wish was his wish too. When Ranji bathed in the backyard, her kozhundan drew water for her from the well. His mother, Ranji's mother-in-law, would holler, 'Elei, low-born scumbag, what work does a boy have in a place where a woman is bathing?'

'No, athai, it was I who asked him to draw up some water…' Ranji would rush to his defence. After all, how could Ranji, who understood everyone's heart, fail to grasp her brother-in-law's affection for her? There were many such small, everyday happenings that the two of them could look back on—happenings that brought out their mutual affection. To the kozhundan, his madini was his whole world. And Ranji, who cared for his happiness, acknowledged his attentions with a smile.

Even as the schoolmaster was talking excitedly about something, a woman opened the door slightly, stuck her head out to say, 'It's a girl…' and shut the door once again. This was followed by loud ululations and the piercing cries of the new born. Ranji's kozhundan jumped up from the cot in a fit of excitement and cried out happily, 'Haiyya, madini has delivered a baby!' In a little while, water trickled out through the drain hole into the furrow he had dug and he smiled to himself on seeing that. Philomi came out shortly, her face wet with perspiration, bearing a plate filled with sugar, fruit, betel and nuts and handed it around to everyone.

'Ah-ha! So Philomi's friend has delivered a child!' the schoolmaster said, winking. In reply, Philomi nodded happily and extended the plate to him.

'You know something? I'm entitled to twice the share of sweets. First as an acquaintance, then as the soon-to-be teacher of this new born child. So, twice the share.'

Everyone laughed heartily. Even the women who peeped through the door laughed. 'Yes, yes, you can have both shares.' Philomi laughed. Her laughter was filled with the old lively sparkle that she had lost all these days. No one seemed to have noticed it, though.

***

The schoolmaster owned a bit of land in the village. He toiled on it whenever he was free from school work. He had installed a pump set there, lately, and water gushed from it all over the land. It was all owing to Philomi's persuasion. The land had lain barren all these years. The schoolmaster had more or less forgotten that he owned such a piece of land. Everyone remarked that nothing green could possibly spring up in that sandy tract close to the sea. Nonetheless, he topped up the soil with a cartload of fine loam brought down from another village and also dug a well. The ground now wore a carpet of pale green and those tiny saplings, fluttering and dancing in the breeze, made such a wonderful sight.

Philomi went to this plot everyday with the schoolmaster. She took Cruz along with her. She was full of hope now. She had changed even the reclusive schoolmaster into someone consequential in the eyes of the villagers. Perhaps, it wouldn't be impossible bring about a change in her appachi as well.

The schoolmaster's house now looked tidier and appealing than before – like the houses tended to by womenfolk. It was all Philomi's doing. Shouldn't she engross herself in something or the other so that her heart could forget? In the afternoons, the schoolmaster and Philomi had their meals together. As for the village, it buzzed with all kinds of idle talk at one point in time. Later, it forgot everything.

The sea didn't betray them after all, unlike men. The vallam owners did manage to make a haul, though it wasn't as good as it was previously. The launches returned ashore, their bellies filled, like a woman about to deliver. Ruined by debt, some families on the north street left the village for good. Nobody could make out whether those confounded machines roved the sea to brighten their lives or if they roared about, intent on wrecking their very existence. That venerable old man, Pavulu Paatta, learnt to bear everything, though with unutterable anguish.

The sea loves the shores. It sweeps up to Periya Mamiya's hut, in a bid to quench its amorous longings. It has been harbouring an insatiable love for the shores, for hundreds of years now, through countless seasons. If the sea were to throw a tantrum, men could hardly survive it. That the paravars kept forgetting this, was Pavulu Paatta's greatest sorrow.

One day, when it was twilight, Samidas came to Philomi's house. He somehow liked the twilight hour. That was why he always came to see her when twilight fell.

Just the previous day, Philomi had decided to shift permanently to the schoolmaster's house with her appachi after the Sunday service at the church that week. When she had told the schoolmaster about this, he had replied, 'If that's Philomi's wish, I'll stand by it.' That was enough for her. She didn't fear anyone or anything else. Samidas came to see her the following day at twilight.

As he entered the house, she kept looking at him for a moment, then quickly recovered herself and greeted him, 'Come in…'

He walked in unsurely, his head lowered. She couldn't understand how all of a sudden those legs could feel so hesitant about entering that house.

'Come in. This isn't some stranger's house. It's your own Philomi's house.'

He was lost for words, as if they had fled somewhere and hidden themselves. Philomi sensed his helplessness. She looked at the corner where the wicker baskets stood. One of her saris lay folded on top of the baskets. Suddenly, it all came back to her – the day she had lain with him right there. She remembered everything – her anxiety that her ammai might return home and find them together and how they had been bursting with ecstasy like the sails of vallams that billowed out like an umbrella in the wind.

'The Lord won't let me go unpunished. I've wronged you, Philomi.'

She was silent. He spoke again, 'You must forgive me… must pardon me.'

'You mustn't talk like that.'

'I'm getting married the day after tomorrow. I felt like seeing you, talking to you, that's why I came. You must come without fail. I shall be only thinking of you. Tell me you'll come...'

Philomi didn't reply. She merely smiled. The smile brought a strange beauty to her face.

'Why do you smile? Will you come?'

'I'll come,' she replied through her smile. He then prattled on and on about all sorts of things. But her heart was no longer there. After he left, she felt all alone in the house. Cruz didn't understand a thing.

Perhaps, there was no wind at sea that day. The waves were low and the sea lay placid.

GLOSSARY

Aiyya:	term used to address an elderly man or a superior; here used to refer to the Lord, as in Yesu Aiyya or Lord Jesus
Aiyyo:	a loud exclamation used to convey a range of emotions like fear, pain, shock, sorrow or sympathy
Akka:	elder sister
Ammai:	mother
Annan:	elder brother
Appachi:	father
Appan:	father; but is sometimes used in annoyance or anger
Athai:	aunt
Dhayam:	a traditional Tamil dice game
Di:	vocative used to address a girl or a younger woman
Ei:	vocative used to address someone younger or inferior
Elei, ele:	vocative used to address a boy or man younger in age

Etee:	vocative used to address or call a girl or woman younger in age
Jamukkalam:	thick floor mat used to sleep or sit on
Kadal Ammai:	Mother Sea
Karuvadu:	dried fish
Karuvai tree:	a thorn tree of medium height, also known as the black babul
Kilianthattu:	a traditional game played by girls
Kombai dog:	a breed of sighthound, native to Tamil Nadu
Kozhundan:	brother-in-law
Kutty:	term used to refer to a small girl or a young woman
Lungi:	cloth sewn together at the ends, usually worn by men around their waist
Madini:	sister-in-law
Mama:	uncle
Mami:	aunt
Manjanathi tree:	Morinda Tinctoria, commonly known as the Indian Mulberry
Marial:	Mother Mary
Musalmaan:	Muslim man
Muthalali:	master
Nethili:	anchovy
Paatta:	grandfather; term used to address an elderly man
Parachi:	woman from the fishing community
Parakudi:	fishing village or hamlet
Paravan:	man from the fishing community

Periamma:	mother's elder sister or father's elder brother's wife
Sayibu:	saheb or a Muslim man of some importance
Sea Mohini:	sea nymph
Tavalai:	huge brass pot
Thaali:	sacred thread worn by married women
Tharaganaar:	middleman or commissioning agent
Thazhampoo:	screw pine flowers
Thinnai:	a veranda or raised platform built adjoining the entrance of a house
Tiruchendur Kadamba Pond:	a pond inside the Tiruchendur Murugan temple; here used to reinforce the vastness of the sea as opposed to the small pond
Uruttu sev:	a savoury or sweet made from chick-pea flour
Vaagai:	albizia lebbeck or the sirissa tree
Vallam:	a traditional wooden fishing boat resembling a canoe
Vei:	vocative used to address an elderly man
Yesu:	Jesus

ABOUT THE AUTHOR

Vanna Nilavan is the pen name of U. Ramachandran, an eminent Tamil writer and journalist. Born in Tirunelveli, Tamil Nadu, in 1949, he began his career as a journalist. He was part of the editorial team of renowned Tamil magazines like *Tuglaq*, *Subamangala* and *Kanaiyaazhi.* He has several novels, short stories, poems, plays, and articles to his credit. *Kadalpurathil* (1977), *Kamba Nathi* (1979) and *Reinees Iyer Theru* (1981) are three of his most celebrated novels. He has won numerous prestigious awards like the 'Ilakkiya Chinthanai' award for his novel *Kadalpurathil* (By the Sea), the Tamil Nadu Government award for his short story collection, *Dharmam,* and the Ramakrishna Jai Dayal Award, New Delhi. He has also written the screenplay for the Tamil movie, *Aval Appadithan.* Many of his works have been translated into English, Hindi, Malayalam and German.

ABOUT THE TRANSLATOR

G. Geetha has a master's degree in English from Loyola College, Chennai. After teaching English at the undergraduate level for ten years, she is now a freelance translator. Hephzibah Jesudasan's 'Putham House', Joe D' Cruz's 'Ocean Rimmed World' and S. Ramakrishnan's 'Whirling Swirling Sky' are her other translations.